# WITCH YOU WELL
## WESTWICK WITCHES COZY MYSTERIES

## COLLEEN CROSS

SLICE PUBLISHING

## ALSO BY COLLEEN CROSS

Westwick Witches Cozy Mysteries

*Witch You Well*

*Rags to Witches*

*Witch and Famous*

*Christmas Witch List*

*Witching Hour Dead*

*Witching for Love on Valentines Day*

Katerina Carter Fraud Legal Thrillers

*Exit Strategy*

*Game Theory*

*Blowout*

*Greenwash*

*Red Handed*

*Blue Moon*

Nonfiction

*Anatomy of a Ponzi Scheme*

# WITCH YOU WELL: A WESTWICK WITCHES COZY MYSTERY

**BE CAREFUL WHAT YOU WISH FOR...**

Dead billionaires are not good for business! That's what Aunt Pearl complains to Cen when the dead body is found in the cozy family inn at Westwick Corners.

Still, it's not Cen's problem. She lives an ordinary life away from her witch-ful family for a reason. She got her ordinary fiancé and her ordinary job as a journalist using no magic whatsoever, and no inconvenient local murder is going to change her comfortable existence.

Even if the entire town is now accusing Aunt Pearl of murdering her guest. Even if her fiancé is acting weird and talking about seeing ghosts. Even if the town's sexy new sheriff, Tyler Gates, treats her like the most hexing of all the witches...

"...A bewitching, supernatural treat. If you love witch cozy mysteries you'll love Cendrine West and her wacky witch family!"

Listen in Audio

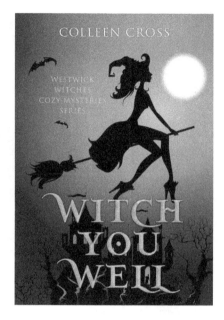

COLLEEN CROSS

WESTWICK
WITCHES
COZY MYSTERIES
SERIES

# WITCH YOU WELL

# CHAPTER 1

*I* had just pulled my ringing cell phone from my purse when Aunt Pearl flew into my newsroom office. And I mean literally flew in—a definite no-no during daylight hours. The fact that we're witches wasn't exactly a well-kept secret in tiny Westwick Corners, but it was best not to flaunt it.

She hovered by the door and frowned. "Cendrine!"

Aunt Pearl only used my full name when angry. Maybe I was angry too. I had been at the office since six a.m. to get caught up. It was almost noon and I was tired, hungry, and sweaty, since my a/c gave up the ghost first thing this morning. My office thermostat read ninety degrees, but I couldn't afford to fix it.

Now what remained of my day was about to be derailed. Well, not if I could help it.

I ignored her as my phone rang. I checked the call display. It was Mom again. She had already called me a half-dozen times this morning with questions about my wedding rehearsal and the grand opening of our family's Westwick Corners Inn, both of which were scheduled for later today. I probably should have just stayed home.

"Cendrine, our new sheriff is a jerk. I want you do an exposé on him." She lingered by the doorway, waiting for my reaction.

"No." I turned away and answered my cell.

Mom was frantic. "Cen, I can't find Pearl. I'm worried she's gone off and done something crazy again."

I pressed the speakerphone button and raised my brows at Aunt Pearl. "She's here with me."

Aunt Pearl approached my desk and yelled into the phone. "I don't need a babysitter, Ruby. I'm perfectly capable of amusing myself."

"That's what worries me," Mom said. "You can't keep running everyone out of town, especially our law enforcement. It isn't right."

"Why don't you just stick a tracking device on me? Sheesh." My aunt slumped into the chair that faced my desk. "I'm not a child."

"You act like one sometimes." Apparently I wasn't the only one who wondered what kind of welcome Aunt Pearl had extended to the sheriff. It was best not to flaunt our specialness. The Wests had been a founding family over a hundred years ago when my great-grandparents had settled in Westwick Corners. But even we could wear out our welcome. There was a limit to what people would put up with.

Aunt Pearl ignored my response. Maybe it was our family's history that gave her such a sense of entitlement. It was too bad, because her flagrant disregard for rules now threatened our continued existence in town. She didn't seem to give a hoot.

She grabbed my phone and yelled into it. "He's trouble, Ruby. Cen's going to do an exposé on him."

I grabbed my phone back. "I'm doing nothing of the sort. What you want and what sells newspapers are two different things, Aunt Pearl. I can't help you. I'm on deadline to get *The Westwick Corners Weekly* published." Like most locals, I had bought myself a job and purchased the newspaper from the retiring owner. Most of the town's industry had dried up when the state highway was rerouted a few years ago. Most young people my age had left for greener pastures shortly after. The few of us that stayed barely eked out a living.

Mom's voice rose. "Now, Cen, Pearl is just trying to help. You take your job too seriously."

Mom's sudden change of tone didn't surprise me. She simply sided with her older sister as a way to minimize collateral damage and keep her own sanity. Mom's coping strategy meant that Aunt Pearl usually got what she wanted, and Mom avoided conflict. As a long-term strategy, I thought it created more problems than it solved.

"Gotta go. See you in a few hours." Mom just enabled Aunt Pearl's bad behavior in her futile efforts to keep the peace. She was oblivious to how Aunt Pearl pushed her buttons to get what she wanted. I, on the other hand, usually stood my ground. The end result was that my aunt and I always butted heads.

Aunt Pearl sank into the chair opposite my desk and snorted. "This isn't a newspaper—it's just an advertorial for bargain hunting coupon clippers. Why do you waste your time? No one reads any of your articles. Face it, Cen. This paper's a dud."

"At least I earn an honest living." Whenever I felt down, Aunt Pearl always made me feel even worse. Her assessment was sadly accurate though. I had bought myself a low-paying, part-time job and wasn't even very good at it. There were few options to make a living in town, so most of us had to be entrepreneurial. "Try saying something nice for a change."

My aunt studied me for a moment but remained silent. She was rarely at a loss for words. I'd better listen to her latest tirade if I wanted to leave the office on time.

She leaned forward. "I'll give you a scoop, so you'll have a decent story for once. Our new sheriff is corrupt and I want you to expose his crimes."

"What crimes?" I checked my watch. It was just before noon. "Sheriff Gates has been on the job what, a few hours? He hasn't even had time to do anything."

3

"He has a past, Cen. A sordid one."

"Don't they all?" Tyler Gates was our fifth sheriff in six months. We attracted only dropouts, deadbeats, and undesirables considered unemployable anywhere else. I was willing to cut him some slack because some law enforcement was better than none. We took what we could get.

"I know why he left his last job." Pearl winked at me. "It's scandalous."

"Oh, really?" The only good thing about the high law enforcement turnover was that it kept my family's supernatural talents more or less secret. The bad thing was that things didn't have to be that way. The main reason for their early departures was the one-woman crime wave that faced me from across my desk.

"Yes, really. One more thing: that highway sign attracts the wrong kind of people." Aunt Pearl's eyes narrowed as she stood to make herself appear bigger. She placed her hands on her hips, ninety pounds of indignation and intimidation.

"It attracts tourists, Aunt Pearl. Just the kind of people we need." Aunt Pearl detested visitors, but unless she stopped her hijinks, Westwick Corners was destined to become just another Washington State ghost town. Our town had no local industry, just aging farmers in the surrounding area who didn't spend much money.

Tourism was our only option, so we had spent months revitalizing and rebranding Westwick Corners as a trendy weekend getaway. I had the sinking feeling that our efforts were about to go up in smoke.

"What's that smell?" I sniffed the air, alarmed that Aunt Pearl's usual stale lavender scent had changed to an acrid gasoline smell. Last time she smelled like a gas station she had gotten on the radar of the Washington State police. Neither the town nor our family needed that kind of attention.

Aunt Pearl smirked but remained silent.

"The whole town voted yes to new highway signs, Aunt Pearl. Sorry, but majority rules." We rarely had visitors anymore since the highway interchange was rerouted to neighboring Shady Creek several years ago. We desperately needed to change that.

"Please don't tell me you damaged the highway sign again."

Silence.

Our property taxes had skyrocketed because of the constant arson and vandalism, and apologies just wore thin after a while. The highway sign wasn't the only thing regularly replaced, and I was tired of the growing ill will towards my family because of Aunt Pearl's misdeeds.

I had a hunch that the highway sign wasn't all she was keeping mum about. "I can smell the gas a mile away. What have you done?"

Aunt Pearl sniffed. "I don't smell anything. Quit changing the subject, Cendrine. That sign hurts my business."

I had no idea why my aunt was mad at me. I decided to tread carefully since pyromania and supernatural powers don't mix well. Magic abilities are both a blessing and a curse. I firmly believed we should harness our magic for the greater good, not wreak havoc.

Aunt Pearl thought otherwise.

"What business?" I blinked as my eyes teared from the acrid fumes.

"Pearl's Charm School."

"Huh?" My aunt was anything but charming.

"My new magic school."

"What magic school? You already have a job at the Inn. You should be there helping Mom right now." Aunt Pearl's new "day" job was officially the housekeeper at the Inn. It was a good way to keep her occupied. Even at seventy years old, she got into tons of trouble when she had too much time on her hands.

"Ruby's got everything under control."

"She sounded kind of stressed out on the phone. I think she could use your help. The guests will start arriving any time now." Our rooms were fully booked, and we had some very important guests.

Tonya and Sebastien Plant, the billionaire couple who had

founded Travel Unraveled, the world's largest travel e-commerce empire, were our VIP guests. Against all odds, they had accepted our invitation to stay at the Inn, which we hoped would result in good publicity. Their experience could make or break our little business venture. It was do or die, so to speak.

"Pearl's Charm School has a grand opening too." Aunt Pearl sniffed as a business card materialized in her hand. She handed it to me. "You should enroll. Heaven knows you could use a magic refresher. No wonder your skills are so rusty, since you never practice. School starts tomorrow, nine a.m. sharp."

"This is bad timing, Aunt Pearl." I turned the business card over in my hand and a witch inside the holograph waved at me. I dropped it face down on my desk.

"No time like the present, especially at my age. I'll do whatever I like," she said. "I've lived here longer than you. Besides, Pearl's Charm School is part of the town's new branding. It caters to supernatural tourists."

"Witchcraft is not part of the official plan." Our entire town had spent thousands of hours collectively on our new tourism strategy, and Aunt Pearl was about to sabotage it all.

All the town's buildings, including the Inn, had been restored to their former glory days of the early 1900s. The only thing not resurrected was the burlesque theater, though we had future plans for live theater.

Few people knew that Westwick Corners was situated on one of the earth's major vortexes, or energy centers. Whether you believed in it or not, it was a good tourist draw. The vortex was what had drawn the West family here in the first place. Until now it had been a well-kept secret.

Now that times had changed and the whole town was fighting for its survival, we decided to capitalize on the vortex. We promoted a New Age theme, complete with a spiritual healing center, spa, and earth energy-themed gift shops.

But not witchcraft.

"You don't even have a place to teach these classes."

My aunt raised her brows and smirked. "Not true. I just rented the old schoolhouse."

"You can't practice magic in plain sight." The schoolhouse was only a few hundred feet from the Inn, and clearly visible from Main Street. I shuddered to think of Aunt Pearl performing magic in plain sight of tourists. It was a recipe for disaster.

"It's a free country." Aunt Pearl sniffed. "I'll do what I like. Most people around here know about our talents."

That was sort of true. Secrets are hard to keep in Westwick Corners. It's a small town where everybody knows each other. The rest of the town didn't really know the true extent of our supernatural abilities though. They had some vague notions of herbal potions and pagan rituals, but beyond that didn't know a whole lot, which was best for everybody concerned. The thought of Westwick Corners morphing into the equivalent of a witch college town would ruin the delicate balance of our fragile existence.

We have a "don't ask, don't tell" policy. The rest of the town doesn't ask and we don't tell. It works better that way. I wanted to get off on the right foot with our new sheriff, and flaunting our magic was sure to have the opposite effect.

I sighed. "You'll need a business license first. Are you really going to list it as a magic school?"

Aunt Pearl scowled and changed the subject. "You young people today don't appreciate your heritage. You, for instance. You've abandoned your craft to kill time at this dump."

"*The Westwick Corners Weekly* is not a dump. It's a hundred-year-old newspaper." I threw my hands up in exasperation as I scanned my shabby office. Renovations remained out of reach unless and until my paper earned more advertising revenue. That wouldn't happen without a jump start to the local economy.

Aunt Pearl scoffed. "Everything in here looks a hundred years old. At least that part is true."

"It's a newspaper, not a showroom." Aunt Pearl had a way of

dismissing my accomplishments. I had let my heart rule my head in thinking I could rescue the paper, but I didn't exactly have other alternatives. *The Westwick Corners Weekly* wasn't *The New York Times*, but it was mine, and I usually beat the rumor mill to a good story.

"Suit yourself. But I can't guarantee the safety of all these mortals you've got visiting. My students need to practice on real people."

"We all agreed to this, Aunt Pearl, including you." I was afraid to ask what she meant by practicing on people, but now wasn't the time. "Complain all you want, but we need tourists. I doubt you even have any students enrolled."

"Want to put money on that, missy? My class is almost full."

She was almost certainly lying, but I wasn't taking chances. "I hold you personally responsible for the safety and well-being of our guests." My future rested on Westwick Corners' growth and prosperity. Otherwise why was I still here?

Brayden Banks was one reason. My fiancé was the town mayor, so we couldn't exactly move away. Our wedding was two weeks away and my future was pretty much mapped out for me.

"The heck you will." Aunt Pearl turned and stormed out of my office. The downstairs door slammed just as Aunt Pearl disappeared into the hall. She abruptly reappeared a few seconds later and walked briskly to my office.

A broad-shouldered man in his late twenties followed behind Aunt Pearl. My mouth dropped open as I recognized the beige uniform that accentuated his athletic build. This new sheriff looked nothing like the middle-aged, balding, pot-bellied men before him. Based on his brisk gait, he was already on the job.

"Now what?" I had a sinking feeling that his visit had everything to do with my pyromaniac aunt who now stood before me, breathless.

"I'll make you a deal," Aunt Pearl said. "You help me with the sheriff, and in return I'll give you a free-ride scholarship for Pearl's Charm School."

"Absolutely not. No deals, and I am not enrolling in your stupid magic school." As soon as the words were out of my mouth I regretted them. But luckily Sheriff Gates was thirty feet away and out of earshot.

Aunt Pearl eyed me up and down and shook her head slowly. "If your grandmother could see you now, she would be mortified at your attitude and your rusty magic. If anyone needs my charm school, it's you, Cendrine."

Technically Grandma *could* see me, since she materialized as a ghost whenever she felt like it. Grandma Vi had been quiet lately as she dealt with her own issues. She was unhappy that her ancestral home had been transformed into the Westwick Corners Inn. Change was hard for all of us.

"I don't need your school. I've got more important things to deal with."

Aunt Pearl snorted. "What could be more important than magic?"

My eyes darted to the approaching sheriff, but he was still fifteen feet away. Aunt Pearl was oblivious to anyone's activities other than her own, as usual.

"Saving our town, for one. We've worked so hard to save this town from turning into a ghost town."

Aunt Pearl shrugged. "What's wrong with a ghost town? I'm tired of all these interlopers. I want some peace and quiet for a change."

Most of the turmoil stemmed directly from Aunt Pearl's actions. Half the town wanted to banish my pyromaniac aunt, and apparently our new sheriff had designs on her too. "Anything you want to tell me before he gets here?"

"No." Aunt Pearl's right eye twitched, a sure sign she was hiding something. Witch or not, no amount of magic could mask her deception.

"That highway sign better be intact, Aunt Pearl. You promised me you wouldn't do anything illegal."

"I didn't promise anything of the sort. Besides, even if I did, I had my fingers crossed." Aunt Pearl's flabby arms jiggled as she waved her hand in the air.

I rolled my eyes. "We'll discuss this later."

"Am I interrupting something?" Sheriff Tyler Gates stood in the doorway. He was hard to miss, not that I wanted to. His dark wavy hair skimmed the top of the doorframe as he paused at my office door. My heart skipped a beat as my gaze met his chocolate brown eyes. Suddenly Westwick Corners didn't seem so boring after all.

I stood, transfixed by his infectious smile. I held out my hand. "Sheriff, thanks for stopping by. Welcome to Westwick Corners."

"Call me Tyler. This place is too small to be formal." He took my hand and shook it.

I felt a catch in my throat as our eyes locked. "I hope you'll like it here." My face flushed as I stared shamelessly at the best-looking man I had ever laid eyes on.

The sheriff carefully sidestepped Aunt Pearl. "I had planned to drop in later in the week, but something's come up." He tilted his head towards my aunt.

"Oh?" His uniform clung to his muscular chest in all the right places. "If it's Aunt Pearl, she can be a bit over the top sometimes."

I felt a tug at my sleeve.

"Don't talk like I'm not even here." Aunt Pearl leaned in, putting herself between the sheriff and me. "That's what I came to talk to you about. The sheriff—"

I coughed as I inhaled my aunt's eau de gasoline fumes. "I'm not bailing you out this time, Aunt Pearl. If you've done something, own up to it."

I turned to Tyler. "I'm sure we can fix whatever it is." As the town's sole journalist, I wanted a good working relationship with the town's only law enforcement.

Yeah.

Aside from being so damn hot, Tyler Gates seemed pretty normal. In fact, way too normal for Westwick Corners. He was about my age, unusual compared to his middle-aged predecessors who arrived in Westwick Corners only as a last-ditch stop when no one else would hire them. But the fact he was even here meant Tyler Gates was damaged goods. His issues just weren't visible on the outside.

I turned back to my aunt. "What did you do that you're not telling me?"

"That's what I've been trying to tell you, Cen. Listening has never been one of your strong points." She leaned closer and whispered. "I had to use a little magic."

I glared at her.

"You had to use what?" Sheriff Gates furrowed his brows and bent slightly. "I didn't catch that."

My heart almost stopped. This was one secret we had to keep.

"A hatchet," I said. "She used a hatchet to cut the sign. Isn't that what you said, Aunt Pearl?" It had to be that damn sign. She just wouldn't let it go.

My arsonist aunt shrugged. The corners of her mouth turned up ever so slightly, amused at my bad rhymes.

Sheriff Gates looked confused. "The sign was torched, not chopped. I'm not quite following."

I waved him away. "Aunt Pearl gets a bit confused sometimes."

"I do not!" Aunt Pearl stamped her foot. "I'm sharp."

I glared at her, then turned to smile sweetly at the sheriff. "She won't do it again, I promise."

Aunt Pearl snapped her fingers at the sheriff.

"Do what?" A split second later he froze in suspended animation.

"Aunt Pearl! Take that spell off him!" I was horrified at her flagrant disrespect for our new sheriff. "You talk about my magic! What you did is an abuse of power."

Aunt Pearl winked as she snapped her fingers twice in quick succession. "Too late."

The Sheriff teetered slightly then regained his balance as the spell lifted.

"It's never too late for justice." Sheriff Tyler Gates winked back at her, his nose crinkled from the fumes. "I think I'm really going to like this place."

"You are?" we both replied in unison.

"You bet I am." He reached into his shirt pocket and pulled out a notepad. He scribbled something with his pen before he tore it off and handed it to Aunt Pearl. "Less than one day on the job and I'm already earning my keep."

Aunt Pearl's smile vanished as she read the paper. She dropped it on my desk. It was a five-hundred-dollar fine for public mischief.

This sheriff meant business.

I liked him already.

# CHAPTER 2

*A* cool, late-summer afternoon breeze softened the swelter. I drove with the windows open, relishing the breeze.

Summer is my favorite time of year, but I also love the promise of fresh new beginnings that autumn brings. The approaching change of season promised a new start in more ways than one. Tonight's Westwick Corners Inn grand opening ushered in our new family business, and two weeks after that was my wedding, when I would start a new chapter in my life.

Instead of excitement I felt heaviness in my chest. I just assumed we would do the happily ever after thing like everybody else. But everything changed earlier this year when Brayden became the youngest-ever mayor of Westwick Corners. His political ambitions now seemed to trump any time we spent together. He constantly canceled our plans to attend one networking event after another. I wasn't cut out to be a political wife, but it seemed too late to do much about that now.

I didn't even have anyone to talk to about it. All my friends had left town soon after high school to attend college or work in Seattle or further afield. In fact, any place other than boring little Westwick

Corners. Brayden and I were the only ones in our graduating class to stay. Everyone else in town was married with kids. The few singles in town were mostly my relatives. Witches aren't all that big on marriage, but I digress.

I probably would have moved away too if I wasn't with Brayden. I made that choice freely, but I missed hanging out with my girl-friends. At least I would see most of them at my wedding in a few weeks' time.

I drove up the winding tree-lined driveway and reached the hill-top. Our rural property sat above the town on a hill that overlooked the valley. The Westwick Corners Inn was formerly our family home, a stately mansion surrounded by a vineyard and a formal garden. Like everyone else in town, we needed a way to earn a living, so we planned to operate the Inn as a sort of country bed & breakfast as a way to support ourselves.

Our newly renovated property also served as my wedding venue. Brayden and I would exchange our vows in the garden gazebo. Today's rehearsal was a quick run-through, mostly to satisfy my perfectionist mom that we would get hitched without a hitch.

I parked and glanced towards the Westwick Corners Inn as I crossed the driveway towards the garden. The Inn's twelve suites included two private suites on the ground floor for Mom and Aunt Pearl. I lived in a separate self-contained tree house at the rear of the property.

My charming cottage in the trees had been custom-built by my grandfather for my grandmother more than a half-century ago. It probably sounds like a children's playhouse, but my hideaway was much grander than that. It was a thousand square feet on two levels, built right into and around the massive oak tree that supported it. It was the best of both worlds; close but not too close to my eccentric family. I felt sad that I would be leaving it once I moved in with Brayden after our wedding.

My heart sank when I pulled into the parking lot and noticed that Brayden's BMW was conspicuously absent. The road leading up the hill to our property was completely devoid of traffic too. I was annoyed that Brayden couldn't at least arrive on time for our wedding rehearsal. His late arrivals just wasted other people's time, and it annoyed me to always be waiting for him. Mom would be unhappy to have her schedule messed up on such a busy day too. I hated making excuses for him and feared he might even be late on our wedding day.

I was actually a few minutes early, so maybe I was being unfair. I walked through the formal rose garden and inhaled the delicate scent on the way to the gazebo. The garden was in full bloom, a perfect setting for our ceremony.

The gazebo's exterior was partially covered with several varieties of lush clematis vines that wound around the pillars and provided partial shade. Large white blossoms were interspersed with smaller star-shaped pink flowers, creating a carpet of blooms.

Mom and Aunt Pearl were already at the gazebo; their voices drifted towards me as I drew near. They stood just outside, where Mom busily reattached a vine that had worked its way loose while Aunt Pearl watched. I was a little surprised to see my aunt, since she wasn't one to fuss over weddings and such. Mom had probably enticed her to come along just to keep her out of trouble.

Mom looked up and waved to me as I approached. She was short, like Aunt Pearl, but that's where the similarities ended. Aunt Pearl was flesh-and-bone compared to Mom's plump figure, the result of always double and triple-testing her cooking and baking. Today Mom seemed frazzled from ticking items off her to-do list. The Inn's grand opening, my upcoming wedding, and her perfectionist tendencies were stressing her out. "We thought you were stuck in traffic or something."

Traffic jams in Westwick Corners were unheard of. It was just Mom's non-confrontational way of berating me for making her wait. Mom never said things directly, especially not negative things. She kept her emotions bottled up and stressed herself out instead of expressing herself and possibly upsetting someone. It was her way of not making waves. It wasn't all that effective since keeping the peace just gave her migraines instead.

As I drew closer I noticed beads of sweat on Aunt Pearl's forehead. She had to be up to something. What, exactly, was unclear, but I had a feeling I'd soon find out. As if her highway sign pyrotechnics hadn't already caused enough trouble.

I sucked in a deep breath and channeled my inner calm. I wouldn't react to Aunt Pearl no matter what she did. She disliked me marrying the mayor, even though Brayden was my high school sweetheart and she had known him for years. Suddenly he was the establishment, and she held him personally responsible for every rule she disagreed with.

It was a foregone conclusion that we would marry long before he proposed. Everyone else in our graduating class had moved away as soon as they could, so Brayden was pretty much the only single male in town not collecting Social Security. Other than our new sheriff, of course. But Tyler Gates didn't count. He would be gone within months, just like the other sheriffs before him.

Aunt Pearl and law enforcement didn't mix. She had run half a dozen sheriffs out of town directly as a result of her antics. Her magic and authority figure issues were a catastrophic combination for law and order. At least, until now. I flashed back to the moment earlier today when Sheriff Tyler Gates had fined Aunt Pearl. Those warm brown eyes never wavered. He wasn't bad to look at, either.

"Cendrine!" My aunt's cackle shattered my reverie. "Pay attention!"

Uh-oh. She was still mad at me.

I quickened my pace.

"Huh?" I hadn't done anything except side with Sheriff Gates on shutting down her pyrotechnics. It wasn't often that I got under her skin. I had to admit that it gave me a small sense of satisfaction.

"I haven't got all day. Get your butt over here," Aunt Pearl snapped. "I've got to stand in for that no-good boyfriend of yours. Real men don't leave their women standing at the altar. It's a bad omen. I keep telling you, but you don't listen. You're better off single."

"You only see all the bad, not his good side." For all her snappiness, Aunt Pearl really just wanted the best for me. At least that's what I told myself.

She raised her brows. "I don't like his good side, bad side, or any other side. None of us do. He's AWOL at his wedding rehearsal? Really, Cen. Dump him while you can."

Mom shrugged and held up her hands as she stood slightly behind Aunt Pearl.

Aunt Pearl turned to Mom. "Ruby, you're getting a no-good son-in-law."

"Now Pearl, I'm sure he has a good reason to be late. Besides, Cen's marrying him, not you." Mom stepped between us like a referee at a prizefight. It wasn't easy being peacekeeper in a family of strong-willed witches. "Brayden's already a part of the family, whether you like it or not. He's got some wonderful qualities."

As usual, Mom's words had a calming effect, and we both fell silent. I breathed a sigh of relief. Though I had twenty pounds on my ninety-pound aunt, she could outwit, out-trick, and out-magic me a hundred times over. I didn't stand a chance.

"We've got to wrap this up. The first guests are arriving in less than an hour." Mom wrung her hands as we headed towards the gazebo steps.

"Brayden called to say his meeting ran overtime. He'll be here in a few minutes." It was a lie but it was easier than the truth.

"Let's use a stand-in. He can take over when he gets here," Mom said.

"But who—?" I followed her gaze to my cranky aunt. "Oh no. I am not marrying her."

Mom waved her hand. "It's just a rehearsal, Cen."

"But why rehearse without the groom? I don't see the point."

"Haven't got all day, Cendrine." Aunt Pearl tapped her watch.

COLLEEN CROSS

"Ruby's right. Got things to do, places to go. Want my services or not?"

I didn't want to give in, but they were right. Brayden should be here but he wasn't. I felt pathetic making excuses for him, but I didn't want Aunt Pearl to dislike him more than she did already.

Mom stepped in. "Stop stirring up trouble, Pearl. The only place you have to be is right here, supporting Cen at her rehearsal."

Technically it wasn't my rehearsal, since our wedding party and the marriage commissioner weren't here. Mom had insisted on a pre-rehearsal rehearsal. The absent groom only irked her perfectionist sensibilities.

I was angry with Brayden too. So what if it was a rehearsal of a rehearsal. Our wedding was just weeks away. Didn't I rate enough for his physical presence? I hated playing second fiddle to his political schedule and ladder-climbing.

"Places, ladies." Mom clapped her hands and ascended the gazebo steps. I fell in behind and followed her up the stairs into the gazebo.

She stopped at the top of the stairs and motioned us inside.

I barely noticed. My eyes remained locked on the still empty road, wondering where Brayden was. The next few seconds were a blur as my foot hit something heavy and I tripped and fell backwards.

"What the hell?" Aunt Pearl screamed as she fell on top of me.

"I can't breathe!" Ninety pounds of bone and skin pressed down on my chest. I pulled my arms free and struggled to shift my weight. But I was pinned to the floor.

"Oh my god, he's dead!" Mom shrieked as she pulled Aunt Pearl off me. "There's a body in the gazebo!"

I instinctively rolled over, only to face a bloodied corpse. A dead man's face was just inches from my own.

I screamed and rolled the opposite way as fast as I could, hitting the gazebo wall. I scrambled to my feet and ran to the farthest corner where Mom and Aunt Pearl cowered. We all stared at the scene before us.

An obese man lay belly up on the floor of the gazebo. His face was so covered in blood that he was unrecognizable. A pool of blood stained his clothes and seeped out from under his body.

"Oh my gawd." Aunt Pearl gagged and turned away. A second later she turned back. "Never seen him before. He must not be from around here."

My mouth dropped open as I recognized him. "That's Sebastien Plant of Travel Unraveled. Our VIP guest."

Aunt Pearl now crouched by his body and checked for breathing or a pulse. "Uh-oh."

Mom nodded slowly as realization set in. "He hasn't even checked in yet."

"More like he's checked out." I pulled my cell phone from my pocket and punched in the Sheriff's number. We needed help and needed it fast.

# CHAPTER 3

$\mathcal{T}$en minutes later we waited outside the gazebo as Sheriff Tyler Gates inspected the crime scene. As I tried to digest Sebastien Plant's demise, I realized we still had to attend to our soon-to-arrive guests in addition to the recently departed one. I glanced down at my brand-new white linen dress, now stained with blood. I shuddered to think that I had been lying atop a corpse just minutes earlier.

I walked over to the foot of the stairs and peered inside. Sheriff Gates walked around the body, deep in thought. I opened my mouth to speak but was interrupted by the sheriff.

"You know him?" Tyler Gates knelt alongside Sebastien Plant's body.

"Not personally. He's Sebastien Plant, one of our guests," I said. "Or rather, would have been. He was supposed to stay with us but hadn't checked in yet. He is—or was—the billionaire CEO of Travel Unraveled, the global travel empire. We invited him to our grand opening."

I turned to face Mom and Aunt Pearl who had also inched closer to get a better look. Sebastien Plant lay on his back, his large belly pointed upward like a beached whale.

Mom buried her face in her hands. "Everything's ruined. No one will ever visit our inn again. How can we possibly salvage our business?"

"Relax," Pearl quickly averted her gaze from the body lying on the floor. "He probably had a heart attack. Just look at him. He obviously didn't take good care of himself."

"With all that blood?" I shook my head. "That's no heart attack." Sebastien Plant was morbidly obese, but his bloodied head told me that he died from something other than poor lifestyle choices.

"How can I possibly relax?" Mom's voice broke as she grabbed onto my arm for support. "That poor, poor man. I can't believe he lost his life in our garden."

"We'll find out who killed him," Aunt Pearl said. "But you can just forget about these stupid tourism plans. Nobody will want to visit here now."

"We still don't know how he died." Aside from his bloodied head he had scratches on his arms and face. Judging by his injuries, he had sustained multiple hits and had tried to defend himself. I shuddered to think we had a killer in our midst.

Sebastien Plant's death was very tragic. It was also very poorly timed for the Westwick Corners Inn grand opening. I took a few steps back from the gazebo. "Let's give the sheriff some room."

"How will we keep the guests away from the gazebo?" Mom's eyes darted back and forth between me and the gazebo as she wrung her hands.

"The sheriff must have a plan. I'm sure he's dealt with this sort of thing before." This sort of thing being a crime scene, I tried not to let my own worries show. Gaining and losing the attention of billionaire Sebastien Plant, the globe-trotting travel tycoon, all in the space of a week brought out a roller-coaster of emotions for me too.

"Who's the killer?" Aunt Pearl's eyes narrowed. "Are there other victims?"

Sheriff Gates shook his head as he emerged from the gazebo. "I haven't heard of any other deaths. We won't know the official cause of death until the crime techs process the scene and the coroner does an autopsy. I've called in the Shady Creek police to assist me."

Shady Creek was about an hour away. It sprang up out of the foothills about twenty years ago and had grown rapidly since the highway was rerouted away from Westwick Corners. As Westwick Corners businesses dried up, we became increasingly reliant on Shady Creek for things like medical treatment, courts, and anything beyond basic police services.

"Some expert you are. It's obviously a murder." Aunt Pearl's voice was flat, like she had an inside scoop or something.

The sheriff sighed. "I can't comment on the cause of death, but it certainly looks suspicious. Only the coroner can tell us what happened for certain though, so let's not jump to conclusions."

While the sheriff consoled Mom, I stepped behind him and peered into the gazebo. Now that I was over my initial shock, I wanted a better look.

Sebastien Plant's body lay like a surreal still life amongst the floral wedding decorations that twisted around with blooming clematis on the poles and railings. His bruised and bloodied head looked like he had been in an extremely bad bar fight. However he had died, it wasn't from natural causes.

My mouth dropped open and a shiver ran down my spine. Aunt Pearl's wand rested atop Sebastien Plant's chest. She must have dropped and forgotten it with all the confusion. Yet I had never known Aunt Pearl to forget much of anything, especially not the wand that never strayed from her side.

It didn't take a genius to see that Sebastien Plant's death resulted from blunt force trauma. Aunt Pearl's wand on his chest certainly looked suspect. Why hadn't she taken it?

The evidence was incriminating, but explainable. Her wand had probably slipped from her hand when she tripped and fell. I couldn't remember her holding it when I arrived at the gazebo, though she must have had it. Everything happened so fast that it was a bit of a blur.

I was more concerned that Aunt Pearl would take it upon herself to explain what it was, which was even worse. This new sheriff was oblivious to our supernatural tendencies. It was better for everyone if we kept things that way.

I glanced over at Aunt Pearl who quickly averted her eyes. She seemed unconcerned that her wand rested on a dead man's chest. At any rate, it was too late to retrieve it. I looked back at the wand and noticed for the first time the wand's bloodied tip. The sheriff noticed it too, at the very moment I stepped past him.

"Don't go any further," Sheriff Tyler Gates said. "We need to contain the crime scene."

A square of white caught my eye. "What's that?" I pointed to the neatly folded paper that rested beside his body. I hadn't noticed it initially. "The killer left a note."

The sheriff brushed past me and headed back into the gazebo. He knelt beside the body. He lifted the note with tweezers and carefully opened it.

I followed, ascending the stairs slowly so I didn't draw his attention. I remained at the entrance and watched him carefully unfold the paper with the eraser end of a pencil. He took pains not to touch anything but the edges even though he wore gloves.

"Maybe the killer meant only to scare him, not kill him." I stepped closer and crouched down beside the body for a closer look.

"You shouldn't be doing that." The sheriff waved me away. "You'll contaminate the evidence."

"I think I already have." I shuddered to think that I had been lying on top of our recently departed guest just minutes earlier.

"Aren't you going to read the note?" I was dying to know what it said. I tilted my head sideways and silently mouthed the message.

The block letters were printed with a fine black felt pen. The printing was neat and symmetrical, like a child's practiced penmanship. The message was as clear as the precise printing:

*THOUGH YOU TRAVEL FAR and wide,*
*You'd be best to run and hide,*
*Your business was built on travel,*
*But it is here that you become unravelled,*

*YOU HAVE no business staying here,*
*Not to taste our food, nor drink our beer*

*LEAVE WESTWICK CORNERS ALONE,*
*And while you still can, go back home.*

*HANDS off our town and land*
*If you do not,*
*You will be caught*
*And never ever walk this earth again.*

"A RHYME," Pearl shimmied in beside me. "A darn good one, too."

Aunt Pearl rarely complimented anyone. While the tone was playful, the message was not. The poem verse was a direct threat to Sebastien Plant and his company, Travel Unraveled.

"Why warn a victim who is already dead?" I couldn't think of any locals capable of murder, or for that matter, anyone outside of my immediate family who even knew about our VIP guests. "There are other ways to run people out of town."

"So I've heard." Sheriff Gates stood and looked pointedly at Aunt Pearl who had stepped forward for a closer look. "You all have to back off. Outside the crime scene."

"There's no yellow police tape," Aunt Pearl pointed out.

He sighed. "The whole gazebo is the crime scene. Now please leave before you contaminate the evidence." He carefully refolded the paper and placed it into a plastic bag.

"But we were already in there." Aunt Pearl placed her hands on her hips. "You sure you know what you're doing, Sheriff?"

I placed a hand on my aunt's shoulder and guided her to the stairs. I squeezed her shoulder as I whispered in her ear. "Would you please just stop? You're making a terrible first impression."

"What difference does it make? He'll be gone in a month. The tourists won't be back either. At least some good will come of all this." She muttered something else under her breath that I couldn't hear.

I followed Aunt Pearl down the stairs to the garden. "Killing guests is a pretty extreme measure to deter tourism, but Sebastien Plant is famous. It might even draw more tourists."

"Don't be ridiculous." Aunt Pearl's eyes widened. "Nobody will want to come here anymore. It's dangerous."

"Plant's murder will generate tons of publicity, Aunt Pearl. The gazebo could even end up being a shrine of sorts. Sebastien Plant is —or was—a celebrity. His die-hard fans might make a pilgrimage to his final resting place." Plant was hugely popular, with a syndicated television series, magazine, and videos. I didn't believe it myself, but Aunt Pearl might. I was using some reverse psychology on her for a change.

"The man's not even cold and you're already thinking of exploiting him to make money?" Aunt Pearl snorted. "You've got a cold, cold heart, Cendrine."

"Westwick Corners is no Graceland, but I can see how publicity from our VIP guest might be worth more dead than alive. One way or another, it puts Westwick Corners on the map." I turned to Aunt Pearl. "Didn't you forget your wand in the gazebo?"

She frowned but didn't say anything. Her eyes met mine for a second before she turned away and pretended she didn't hear me.

Sheriff Gates descended the stairs and joined us outside. "I don't want you discussing what you saw in there." He pointed to the gazebo. "Especially not the note or the murder weapon."

The sheriff thought Aunt Pearl's wand was the murder weapon? This wasn't looking good. His handsome face betrayed no emotion, which I supposed was all part of the professional detachment of being a cop. I couldn't help wondering if he already regretted coming to Westwick Corners. As the lone sheriff, he was going to be busy.

"Maybe he got killed by accident," Aunt Pearl said. "That would explain the note. You don't threaten someone in a note and then immediately kill them. That makes no sense."

"Maybe the note was left as a warning to his wife," Mom said. "Tonya Plant is part of Travel Unraveled too. The killer wanted them both to leave."

Sheriff Gates nodded. "The killer could be a local who doesn't want the Plants here. Speaking of which, where is his wife?"

I shrugged. "No idea. We had no idea they had even arrived. They haven't checked in yet." The official grand opening was today, with the first guests due to arrive around now.

"Who would do such a thing?" Mom's eyes widened as she noticed my bloodstained dress for the first time.

"Most locals are on board with the tourism plans, but not everyone is. None of the locals are capable of murder though." I looked pointedly at my aunt, who ignored me.

"People do extreme things when they feel threatened." Sheriff Gates stood and waved his hand in the direction of the Inn. "You should all go back inside. Don't leave the property though. I'll want to interview each of you as soon as I hand off the gazebo to the crime scene techs."

"I still don't get it," Aunt Pearl said. "Why threaten Plant when he's already dead?"

A chill ran down my spine. The wand, the note, and everything else pointed to my ornery aunt. If it were that obvious to me, it would be to the sheriff too.

I made a mental note to ask Mom about Pearl's whereabouts prior to the gazebo. I knew she wasn't capable of murder, but she was certainly capable of trouble. She hadn't exactly made a good first impression with the sheriff, so the more we knew ahead of her interview with the sheriff, the better. The investigation could easily get steered in the wrong direction with one of her snide remarks. We needed a strategy.

I followed behind Mom and Aunt Pearl. As we walked across the garden, I glanced toward the parking lot. Still no sign of the police reinforcements the sheriff had called from Shady Creek. By the time they arrived and processed the scene it would probably be after dinner. Since it was still only late afternoon, we had to formulate a plan to keep the crime scene under wraps and out of sight. We also had to keep our guests out of the garden.

I turned to Mom. "The whole idea of a killer in our midst is really creepy. Why would anyone turn people away from our town?"

Aunt Pearl coughed. "I've got to go." She broke away from us and walked briskly towards the Inn. She disappeared into the Inn's basement entrance.

Mom's eyes widened and met mine. "I'd better follow her."

I glanced back at the gazebo where Sheriff Gates stood, arms crossed. His head turned and followed her path across the garden. He frowned as she picked up speed.

The fact that Aunt Pearl had left her wand behind troubled me. She didn't even seem to care about it, though she never went anywhere without it. She walked faster than I had ever seen anybody walk, a blatant use of magic if I ever saw it. She hardly seemed the frail elderly woman she pretended to be about town. It just spelled trouble.

I checked my watch, surprised to see that over an hour had passed since I had arrived at the gazebo. Still no sign of Brayden. Either he had somehow heard about Plant's murder, or he had completely forgotten about our three p.m. rehearsal. Whatever the reason, my future husband couldn't be bothered to show up for either our wedding rehearsal or to comfort me.

# CHAPTER 4

"Wait—don't go yet." Sheriff Tyler Gates' deep voice cut through the silence.

My heart stopped as I looked up and into his soft brown eyes. My pulse quickened and for a split second I forgot I was at a murder scene.

I flushed as I felt his gaze on me. What was I thinking?

I turned around and walked slowly back to the gazebo. I followed him inside.

He pointed in the direction of Plant's body. "You've seen it before, haven't you?"

My shock must have registered on my face. I nodded slowly, still not comprehending why Aunt Pearl's magic wand was in the gazebo in the first place. I knew she hadn't forgotten it since she never let it out of her sight. I flashed back to her hasty exit. It was almost like she was running away from something.

But that wasn't what troubled me most. The top of the five-pointed filigree star was darkened with congealed blood. The sheriff shone his flashlight beam onto the wand, completely unnecessary since even the gazebo had no shadows in the bright afternoon sun.

The bloodstains were clearly visible. "It belongs to Aunt Pearl." I glanced towards the Inn.

"What is it? It looks like half a curtain rod or something."

It was true that the star atop the wand resembled some of the fancier finials for sale at Walmart, but Aunt Pearl's wand was much more dangerous than a curtain rod. Even more so now, since it seemed to have been used in a murder.

"It's her uh...cane." The star tips were sharply pointed, but not enough to inflict the sort of damage I saw before me. Aunt Pearl wasn't strong enough to commit such an act. At least not without magic.

She was also afraid of blood.

"I didn't know she used one."

I opened my mouth but no words came out.

There had to be a logical explanation, though Aunt Pearl herself defied logic. I needed to talk to her before the sheriff did. I know that sounds unethical, but we had to hide our magic at all costs or we'd soon see another sheriff quit our town. Something told me Aunt Pearl was about to cross a line that would change things forever.

Our magic had to stay secret. It was essential for our continued coexistence in Westwick Corners. Aunt Pearl knew that of course, but she had a tendency to act first and cover her tracks later.

"She seems pretty agile," he said. "She obviously doesn't need a cane."

We both watched Aunt Pearl and Mom walk briskly towards the Inn's kitchen door and disappear inside.

"Pearl moved pretty well under her own power on the highway this morning too." Tyler Gates frowned. "I had to sprint to catch up with her. I'd never believe she needed a cane."

"She has occasional bouts of rheumatism."

"Really?" His brown eyes studied me. "She looks pretty limber to me."

I nodded. I hated to lie, but I had no choice until I found out exactly how my aunt's wand had gone AWOL in the first place. She never let it out of her sight. Had she returned to the scene of the crime to retrieve it? That implied that she knew it was here. That didn't make her a murderer, but it didn't explain the blood on her wand either.

I flashed back to the scene. Sebastien Plant's head and face had been covered in so much blood that it was difficult to determine the size of the wound. It was hard to imagine that my aunt's wand could do that much damage. I shuddered as I flashed back to his bloodied face. "I didn't think her wan—I mean cane—was sharp enough to draw blood, let alone kill someone."

"You'd be surprised what people can do in the heat of the moment." The sheriff looked doubtful even as he said it.

"Aunt Pearl is ornery, but she's not a murderer. You don't really think—"

"Doesn't matter what I think. The coroner determines the cause of death. There's no point in speculating until we have her conclusion."

"But there's a logical explanation for all this."

He waved his arm in dismissal. "I've only got one question. Why was Pearl's cane on top of Sebastien Plant's body?"

I frowned. "Aunt Pearl and I tripped over his body." My comment implied that she was holding her wand at the time we both fell, and I didn't try to correct it. I was almost certain she hadn't been holding her wand when we fell onto Plant's body. She would have poked me with it if she had. I didn't want to mislead a murder investigation, but I also wasn't about to incriminate my aunt. "You can't possibly think Aunt Pearl had anything to do with this."

"I go where the facts take me. At the moment they lead to Pearl. At least until she answers my questions."

Sheriff Gates' face remained expressionless, so I couldn't tell whether he was serious or not. I thought back to Aunt Pearl's earlier comment about the sheriff being corrupt. She never gave a reason, but what if there was some basis in truth? If he wanted to solve the case quickly he could easily railroad my aunt. We didn't exactly attract the most upstanding police candidates around, so maybe that was what was wrong with him. Because there was always something wrong with anyone who moved to Westwick Corners. They were either hiding something in their past or hiding from someone.

I pointed to Aunt Pearl's wand. "That pointy tip isn't sharp enough to draw blood, let alone kill anyone. It looks harmless enough to me." Exactly the opposite was true, magic-wise. In the wrong hands, that wand was deadly dangerous. But the sheriff didn't know we were witches and I wasn't about to tell him.

As I stared at the wand I had an epiphany. Aunt Pearl couldn't have possibly killed Sebastien Plant. I flashed back to a few months ago when she had cut her finger and fainted. My tough-as-nails aunt was deathly afraid of blood.

I was certain of one thing. I didn't know how or why, but someone else was responsible for the blood on Aunt Pearl's wand.

Come hell or high water, I would track them down.

# CHAPTER 5

*I* headed into the kitchen, where Mom watched aghast as Aunt Pearl busily tossed a salad—literally—for tonight's dinner. At least she was using her magic constructively for once, though I was surprised at the mess she had made in just a few minutes.

I caught a head of Romaine mid-air and placed it on the counter. "We need to talk."

"I'm busy, Cen. It will have to wait." She snapped her fingers and julienned a tray of carrots.

"Missing something?" I asked.

"Hmmm, carrots, tomatoes, cucumbers...no, I don't think so."

"I meant your wand. Why did you leave it at the gazebo?" Considering that wand never left her side, she seemed awfully nonchalant about it.

"I haven't got time to talk right now. We've got to get dinner ready for the guests." Aunt Pearl stood at the middle island in our large commercial kitchen. The once-gleaming stainless steel was covered in congealed drips and vegetable peelings. The kitchen was the only part of the Inn that had been professionally renovated. We had invested thousands and it was Mom's pride and joy. Right now though, it was a royal mess.

Mom's spotless kitchen had morphed into an epicurean wasteland. The counter was stacked with dishes and dirty pots filled the sink. A burnt smell permeated the humid air. That was the trouble with magic. Disaster took only minutes to create. Either Aunt Pearl's magic had gone haywire, or she had found an outlet to vent.

"A few minutes ago you wanted all the guests gone," I said.

"Well, they're here now. We have to feed them." Aunt Pearl wiped sweat from her forehead with a flour-dusted forearm.

Mom stepped forward and frowned. "I already had everything prepared, Pearl. You're just making a mess in here."

"I didn't think we had enough food, so I made more." My aunt pouted like a scolded child.

I nodded to Mom. "You take care of the food and I'll handle Aunt Pearl."

"No one's 'handling' me, Cendrine. Especially not you."

"Listen to me, Aunt Pearl. Sebastien Plant was just murdered and your wand was lying on his chest. How did it get there?"

Aunt Pearl's mouth dropped open. "So that's where my wand went."

"Don't play dumb with me. You saw it in the gazebo just as I did. Why did you leave it there?"

"I didn't! Someone stole it." She threw her arms up in the air. "I can't pick up something at a crime scene and get my fingerprints all over it. I could be framed!"

"But it's your wand. It already had your fingerprints on it."

"I'm not going to stand here and listen to your accusations." Aunt Pearl tore off her apron and threw it in the air. It landed on the grill and began to smoke just as she turned and stomped towards the door.

I grabbed the apron off the grill and threw it on the floor. I stomped out the embers before running after my aunt. "Wait—Aunt Pearl! No one is accusing you of anything. We just need to know what really happened so we don't expose ourselves." I hoped she wouldn't make up one of her far-fetched stories. I just wanted the truth. Why couldn't she answer the question?

"Now, Cen. I am a lot of things, but I am not an exhibitionist."

I frowned. "You know what I mean. People can't find out we're witches, especially not in the midst of a murder investigation."

"I just don't see how my wand has anything at all to do with that. I'm not a killer." She sniffled and blinked away imaginary tears.

"We know that, Pearl," Mom said. "But the investigation's about to get sidetracked if we don't set the sheriff straight. The more time he spends looking at you, the less time he has to find the real killer. In the meantime a murderer is loose. The sooner the killer is caught, the better for all of us."

That seemed to appease Aunt Pearl. "Sheriff Gates definitely has it in for me. I don't want to be framed."

Our town's small size was a stroke of luck, I realized. The sheriff was on his own, unable to separate us for questioning. We had an opportunity to get our stories straight before the Shady Creek reinforcements arrived. It sounded criminal, but it was vital to keep our magic under wraps.

"Then help us," Mom pleaded. "Tell us everything you know—what you're going to tell Sheriff Gates."

"There's not much to tell, other than how we found him in the gazebo." Aunt Pearl met my gaze and nodded towards Mom. "Ruby and I walked over there together just a few minutes before you arrived, Cen. I already told the sheriff that."

I hadn't even noticed her talking with the sheriff, but I had probably been too preoccupied to notice. "Did he ask you anything else?"

Aunt Pearl shook her head. "He said he might have more questions later on. Some sheriff. He didn't even ask for my DNA."

"Thank goodness," Mom said. "I sure hope he's got a lead. Who would dare to kill the best thing for tourism this town has ever seen?"

I was pretty sure the sheriff hadn't ruled out any suspects yet. Not even silver-haired witches.

Aunt Pearl cleared her throat. "I can't imagine anyone doing that."

I ran through a list in my mind of local troublemakers. We didn't have much crime in our small town, and certainly no violent criminals. All the evidence pointed right back at the person standing next to me. Aunt Pearl *was* the number one town troublemaker. She was capable of a lot of things, but murder wasn't one of them.

My aunt seemed to guess what I was thinking. "Certainly not little ol' me. Though I must admit that I can't think of a better way to permanently deter visitors than killing them."

"Pearl!" Mom shook her head. "Don't talk like that. All we need is for someone to overhear and misinterpret you."

"Why would anyone think I wanted to kill him? I don't even know the guy."

"People jump to conclusions sometimes." Mom shrugged. "As long as you have an alibi, you have nothing to worry about. Someone can vouch for your whereabouts, right?"

I turned to Mom. "Wasn't Aunt Pearl with you?"

Mom's voice broke. "I think we'd better let Pearl speak for herself."

That spelled trouble. Mom never let Pearl speak for herself if she could help it.

"I've got to go." Aunt Pearl turned and left through the back door before either Mom or I could say another word.

Mom sighed. "She's not herself, Cen. I'm afraid of what she'll do next. Once she's got an idea, there's no stopping her."

Aunt Pearl's anti-tourism crusade scared me too. Either she had taken things way too far, or someone had framed her. But who would do such a thing?

# CHAPTER 6

*A*unt Pearl returned as quickly as she had left, but provided no explanation for her sudden departure. She watched in silence as I cleaned up the lettuce debris and Mom transferred the tossed salad into large glass serving bowls. Thanks to Aunt Pearl, we had enough greens to feed a rabbit farm for a year.

"I'm heading upstairs to clean." Aunt Pearl turned on her heels and headed for the door.

"Now?" Mom stared after her.

Mom and I exchanged worried glances.

Aunt Pearl ignored Mom and slammed the door behind her

My spidey senses tingled at the thought of Aunt Pearl going upstairs alone, so I followed her out of the kitchen, keeping far enough back so she remained unaware of my presence. She headed up the large oak staircase towards the second and third floor guest rooms.

I waited until she reached the second floor landing before ascending the stairs. I winced as the stairs creaked, but Aunt Pearl appeared not to notice. I reached the second floor and followed a safe distance behind her down the hallway. She stopped at Tonya

Plant's room at the end of the hall and pulled a giant key ring from her pocket.

Aunt Pearl's housekeeping cart was already parked in the hallway outside the room. I doubted her plans included any sort of cleaning. I had to stop her before she got into more trouble.

"Aunt Pearl—what are you doing?" My whisper sounded more like a rasp.

"Cleaning Tonya's room, of course." She turned to face me. "By the way, you're a lousy sleuth. I knew you were following me the whole time."

I ignored the insult. "Why are you cleaning the Plants' room? They just got here." And poor Sebstien Plant had already checked out.

Aunt Pearl shook her head. "No, I checked them in early this morning."

My mouth dropped open. "Why didn't you mention that to the sheriff? You never corrected Mom when she said they hadn't arrived yet."

She shrugged. "It's no big deal. I just didn't want Ruby to look stupid in front of the sheriff."

"It's a huge deal. Since when do you worry about other people's feelings?" She was lying and I knew it. "You're covering up for yourself."

"Okay, maybe a little. I forgot to fill in all the check-in paper-work and I didn't want Ruby mad at me. The Plants arrived around one a.m. Sebastien was really drunk and could barely stand, so I got them a room quick. I checked them in myself." Aunt Pearl's key ring jangled as she unlocked Tonya Plant's door. She pulled a pair of latex gloves from her housekeeping cart and snapped the wrists as she put them on.

"You should have said something. Had the sheriff known, I'm sure he would have inspected this room. It's a potential crime scene. Just stay here and I'll go get him."

"Oh relax, Cendrine. Sheriff Gates hasn't called it a crime scene yet, and he never will unless we help him find the evidence. He'll never figure it out on his own, which means he'll never check this room in time. It's up to us." She tossed me a pair of gloves. "Put these on. We haven't got all day."

"No, wait." It scared me half to death to think of Aunt Pearl and a crime scene in the same sentence. There was no telling what would go wrong. "This is a mistake. You've got to stop taking matters into your own hands like this."

"Stop your whining and get to work. You can empty the garbage."

Aunt Pearl's vice-like grip closed on my bicep and pulled me inside the room. I yelped in pain but did as I was told. I had no choice. The voices of approaching guests echoed in the hall. They couldn't hear us argue.

"This is a bad idea." I slipped on my gloves and glanced around the room. It seemed undisturbed except for the unmade bed, which looked barely slept in. The couple's luggage sat unopened in the closet. A half-full glass of lemon-lime soda, car keys, and a wallet sat on the nightstand and an empty Walmart bag rested on the desk. Other than that, the room was tidy.

Nothing in the room indicated the demise of one of its occupants. The only strange thing was the full trash can, which seemed odd given the Plants' recent arrival. I lifted the trash can and emptied it into a large black garbage bag. Aside from tissues, the trash can contents included a half-empty Gatorade bottle and a one-gallon plastic container. I tied the bag in a knot, deciding to keep the bag separate from the other rubbish just in case the sheriff wanted to look at it later.

Aunt Pearl beckoned me over. "Look what I found." She pointed at the desk, speechless.

I walked around the bed to see what she was staring at and almost had a heart attack.

My uneasiness at being inside Tonya Plant's room vanished once I saw the development plans and feasibility study laid out on the desk. I recognized the Centralex Development logo. Centralex was the biggest commercial property developer in the Pacific Northwest. Beside the plans were architectural renderings of a mega resort, hotel, and conference center. The neat block printing read *Westwick Resort* and left no doubt where the intended location was.

The aerial photographs and diagrams were clearly of our property. The architectural rendering showed a twenty-storey building with pools, a golf course, and gardens. The Westwick Corners Inn was nowhere in sight.

"Believe me now?"

I nodded, numb from shock. Someone had taken considerable time and expense to develop plans that seemed to include razing our historic inn to the ground. They were so confident about their project that they had hired architects and planners that must have cost tens of thousands of dollars, yet they hadn't even talked to us, the property owners. It seemed a risky bet. It was also very underhanded of the Plants to stay at our property at the very moment they planned to swindle us out of it.

Now I really regretted inviting them. The late Sebastien Plant now appeared more foe than friend. I wondered how quickly he planned to put his plan into action. His murder took on a whole new dimension now that his real reason for coming to Westwick Corners became clear. I shivered at the thought that we were connected, albeit tenuously, to his final moments on earth.

"Progress is a double-edged sword," Aunt Pearl said. "Sometimes it's better to be invisible and ignored."

It was the first time today we'd actually agreed on something. "Let's go find the sheriff," I said.

A few weeks ago we couldn't even find paying guests. Now our guests were ready to pull our business out from under us. Did they want it bad enough to kill for it?

# CHAPTER 7

*S*heriff Gates turned Tonya's room over to the crime scene techs for processing, which didn't go over well with Tonya. She was furious that she couldn't return to her room. The inn was fully booked, so we couldn't even offer her another room for the few hours it took investigators to check it out. Her only option was to cool her heels in the dining room.

I had surrendered the garbage bag from Tonya's room to the sheriff, who handed it over to the crime scene techs to process.

I wished I had ignored Aunt Pearl's orders and called the sheriff immediately. Gloved hands or not, the things we had touched in the Plants' room had potentially tainted them as evidence.

At least the Centralex plans were no longer a secret. Tonya couldn't pretend to be simply enjoying our hospitality while plotting to raze the Inn. Her deceit didn't seem to bother her. Apparently nothing did.

She sat in the dining room with an oversized slab of chocolate cake and a glass of red wine. She seemed to be enjoying herself a little too much considering her husband's recent demise.

The sheriff promised Tonya that she would have her room back shortly after dinner, and it couldn't be soon enough for me. At least I wouldn't have to face her and feign politeness. The sooner she was gone the better, as far as I was concerned.

The sheriff temporarily repurposed a small room off the Inn's front parlor as a private interview room. We had designed the front parlor as a casual lounge-type area for guests to relax, but I was anything but chill as I awaited my turn for questioning.

I was eager to ask the sheriff about the development plans in Tonya's room and whether they factored in to the murder or not. Maybe Tonya had already mentioned their real reason for coming to Westwick Corners, but I somehow doubted that. She didn't seem the type to volunteer information.

My chair by the window gave me a good vantage point of our guests' comings and goings. Most of the guests were relaxing before dinner, and a few had even drifted over to *The Witching Post,* our bar in a separate building, for pre-dinner drinks. Luckily the bar was located on the opposite side of the Inn, so the gazebo and gardens were out of sight. I just hoped the police would confine their activities to the garden area.

My window seat also allowed me to quickly run outside and redirect any guests headed towards the gardens and gazebo. Under no circumstances could they discover that a murder had taken place just steps from where they were staying.

It had only been hours since our morbid discovery in the gazebo, but it seemed like an eternity. The sheriff had guarded the crime scene—or scenes—since it now included Tonya's room—until the arrival of the Shady Creek crime scene investigators. Now that he had debriefed them he focused on witness interviews. That included me, of course, and Mom and Aunt Pearl.

Sheriff Gates had interviewed Mom first, so she was freed up to attend to dinner for the guests. Next came Aunt Pearl. I was both surprised and thankful to see that my aunt's interview lasted all of five minutes.

He had then disappeared to make a quick call, which I assumed was to the on-scene investigators. I hadn't been able to talk with either Aunt Pearl or Mom after their interviews. I just hoped that Aunt Pearl hadn't said anything outrageous or incriminating.

I smiled as he walked over and sat down across from me. "I hope this can be cleared up quickly."

"We'll do our best."

"Can we stay out here? I want to keep an eye on the guests."

He nodded.

I gazed out the front window and was alarmed to see the Shady Creek investigators' white van now parked close to the Inn's front entrance. The Shady Creek Police emblem was plainly visible. So was the black lettering underneath that read *Forensics*. The coroner's van, also white, was parked beside it.

What would I say if the guests noticed and asked questions? The last thing we needed was a scene. At least there were no media onsite, mostly because my newspaper was the only news media in town. Plant's death was big enough to eventually attract the attention of the Shady Creek reporters, but I hoped nightfall and the start of the weekend would delay any news coverage at least until tomorrow when we might have more answers.

Tyler followed my gaze. "They had to move closer for some of their equipment. Just say they stopped in for a meal at *The Witching Post* if anyone asks."

"Good idea." I might have to, since a shiny black sedan had just pulled into the parking lot. A couple exited their vehicle and unloaded luggage from the trunk. They trudged past the coroner's and forensics' vans with their luggage, seemingly oblivious. At least that was a good sign.

"Now, walk me through everything that happened, step-by-step, right up to when you discovered the body." Tyler Gates' warm brown eyes were easy to get lost in. A little too easy. I forced myself to focus on the task at hand.

I recounted the events, omitting the argument with Aunt Pearl. "We were just about to assume our places when we found the body."

It seemed like he was asking me the same things over and over. Then I realized that it was probably an interrogation tactic.

I shivered as it really hit home. Here I was in the middle of the biggest story to ever hit Westwick Corners and instead of getting a scoop, I was being interrogated for a serious crime. I wasn't sure if I was considered a witness, a suspect, or both. All I knew for sure was that my involvement seriously hampered me getting the full story.

"Any idea why the Plants choose Westwick Corners as a holiday destination? Westwick Corners isn't exactly the French Riviera."

Tyler Gates' comment normally would have got my back up, but somehow he made it sound like it wasn't our fault we were a little hick town.

"We invited them about six months ago," I said. "They never got back to us, so I just assumed they weren't interested. I never in a million years thought that they would accept our invitation. But they finally did. Out of the blue, just two weeks ago, with no explanation why it took them so long."

"I see." A slight smile played on his lips as he jotted more notes. "Tell me what you know about Sebastien Plant."

"Nothing more than most people. He founded Travel Unraveled, so he's a self-made billionaire. We had hoped he'd see the potential in the Westwick Corners Inn and maybe feature us in his television show." I told him about the architectural plans in the Plants' room. "We weren't snooping around, but we couldn't help seeing the plans because they were left in plain view on the desk. All we wanted was a little publicity, not for them to buy the place out from under us."

"You sure no one in your family had some talks with them? Maybe someone made a proposal?"

I shook my head. "Absolutely not. We've spent months renovating. We didn't invest our money and sweat equity to have the place torn down for some concrete monstrosity." I jumped to my feet as two Tyvek-clad men pulled a gurney out of the coroner's van. "I sure hope they aren't going to carry the body across the lawn and parking lot in full view of the guests."

"I'm afraid there's no other alternative." He waved at me to sit back down. "Carry on with your story."

I complied. "There's not much else to tell. It's obvious now why the Plants accepted our invitation. They had their eyes on our property."

"Did they make an offer?"

"No, not yet. I guess Sebastien's murder might have changed their plans. At any rate, we're not selling."

"Hmmm."

"You think the plans are somehow related to the murder?"

"Could be."

"What a disaster." I ran my fingers through my hair. "We'll get lots of publicity now, but the wrong kind. Nobody wants to vacation at a place where someone was murdered."

"People forget eventually."

"Not around here they don't." Between Aunt Pearl's arson and Sebastien Plant's murder, Westwick Corners' crime rate had skyrocketed in less than a day. Our town was quickly descending into lawlessness and I was scared of what might happen next.

I told the sheriff everything I knew, including my whereabouts starting from this morning until my arrival at the gazebo earlier in the afternoon. "There's nothing else I can tell you, other than us literally tripping over Sebastien Plant's body." I shivered as I remembered landing on his soft, yet oddly stiff, body.

He remained silent for several more minutes as he wrote in his notepad.

The more time Sheriff Gates spent on his investigation and at the Inn, the more likely he would discover our family secret. But for now, he was oblivious to the fact that we were witches, and I intended to keep it that way. That gave me no choice but to involve myself in the investigation to clear the case up as soon as possible.

"Sebastien Plant and his wife Tonya weren't due to arrive until around now. But as I'm sure Aunt Pearl told you, they actually arrived around one a.m., so she checked them in herself."

Tyler Gates eyes narrowed. "She never mentioned that. Anything else?"

I brushed a stray lock of hair from my eyes. "How long has he been dead?"

He shrugged. "The coroner determines that, but I figure at least a few hours before you found him. Probably happened sometime this morning, before noon."

"Surely someone saw him around the property." I regretted the words as soon as they left my mouth. My aunt's whereabouts before she arrived at my office this morning were unaccounted for, and she seemed to be the only one even aware that the Plants had checked in."Any other leads?"

"We're not releasing any information right now." His warm brown eyes suddenly cooled. "I know you want a story, but I can't give any details yet."

"Not a thing?" Sebastien Plant's murder was only the second murder in Westwick Corners' history, and the first in my lifetime. It was the lead story I had been waiting for, the biggest thing to happen in recent history. It was also much more than a local story, since the victim was a famous business tycoon and celebrity. I wanted to get the scoop ahead of *The Shady Creek Tattler*.

He shook his head. "Sorry, not yet."

"All right. Just let me know if I can help in any way." I had no intention of standing on the sidelines. While he conducted his official investigation, I would do my unofficial one. It gave me the creeps that a murder had taken place on our property and I wanted it solved quickly.

He tucked his notebook into his jacket and stood. "I'll get back to you if I have any questions."

"I'd like to interview you for the newspaper, though."

"You know where to find me." He smiled and despite myself, I smiled back.

# CHAPTER 8

*A*fter helping Mom with Aunt Pearl's kitchen mess, I headed back into the dining room, which had started to fill with guests. Sheriff Tyler Gates was still there, his notebook and papers spread out on the table beside a cup of coffee.

I worried that our guests might wonder why the sheriff was even here. The picture window behind him framed a panoramic view of the parking lot, where the Shady Creek police vehicles were still parked. I had hoped that the crime scene techs would be both fast and discreet, but it didn't look like that was going to be the case.

Our eyes met and he waved me over.

I felt a pang of guilt. What I considered a mess and an inconvenience was the end of poor Sebastien Plant's life. I had never met him in person, and I suddenly wondered where Tonya Plant was. The table she had sat at earlier was empty, but I doubted her room would have been cleared by the police yet. Sheriff Gates must have already interviewed her. I wondered if he knew of her whereabouts.

I glanced outside as he motioned for me to sit down. Still no sign of Brayden's car in the parking lot. I grew worried, since he hadn't even called. What if something had happened to him? Once I was done with the sheriff I would track him down.

I turned my attention back to Tyler Gates. Though he did his best to remain expressionless, I thought I detected a trace of worry.

"Tell me again what happened. Why exactly, were you in the gazebo?"

"A wedding rehearsal." My eyes locked on his chocolate brown eyes. I tried to look away, but I was drawn into the warmest brown eyes I had ever seen. I couldn't help myself. I was mesmerized, even if I was being interrogated.

I felt a pang of guilt lusting after a man that wasn't my fiancé.

I felt a catch in my throat. "Me."

"Uh-huh." Sheriff Tyler Gates scribbled on his notepad. "Right, so you, Pearl, Ruby, and Brayden were in the gazebo. Anyone else?"

"Uh, no." My face flushed. "Brayden wasn't there."

Tyler Gates's mouth dropped open. "The groom missed his own wedding rehearsal?"

"He was running late."

"I see." He scribbled something in his notebook. "What time did he arrive at the gazebo?"

"He didn't." It occurred to me for the first time that, as mayor, Brayden was actually Tyler Gates' boss. Surely the sheriff knew that Brayden wasn't there. He hadn't been at the gazebo, and his car wasn't in the parking lot.

Tyler Gates raised his brows.

"He never showed for the wedding rehearsal." In a weird sort of way I felt vindicated. Someone other than me was questioning Brayden's sense of priorities. It didn't stop me from feeling terrible though. In Brayden's eyes, I rated lower than a city hall meeting.

"That's interesting." He scribbled something on his notepad.

Other words sprang to my mind, but they weren't nearly as nice.

"I know how it sounds, Sheriff Gates. But his meeting was running late and—" My voice caught in my throat as I realized the enormity of the situation. "He's the mayor. It would look bad if he left the meeting early."

He looked up from his notepad and studied me, but didn't say a word. As an interrogation technique it was very effective, at least on me.

"What meeting was he at?"

"The weekly crime meeting, I think." My face flushed.

Sheriff Gates scribbled more notes as the corners of his mouth turned up ever so slightly. "You mean the weekly crime watch meeting? That got canceled today."

"Oh." Of course Tyler Gates would know about a meeting attended by both mayor and sheriff. Brayden had lied to me. My face flushed in anger and embarrassment.

But if the meeting was canceled, why had Brayden been a no-show?

A trace of a smile played on Tyler Gates' lips. Even the sheriff didn't take me seriously. I had to admit it sounded stupid to me too. I really felt like giving Brayden a piece of my mind.

His expression softened slightly. "I'm sure Brayden had something unexpected come up. And call me Tyler. This town's too small for anything other than first names."

I didn't want to make excuses for Brayden but thought my words needed clarification. I didn't want the sheriff to get the impression that Brayden had just blown me off. "It wasn't actually our final rehearsal. My mom Ruby is a bit of a perfectionist. Today was a pre-rehearsal rehearsal." It didn't justify Brayden's absence, but it was an important distinction.

"I see."

I didn't think he did. "Mom's a worrier. A pre-rehearsal just ensures things go off without a hitch."

"Definitely not the case here. When's the wedding?"

"Two weeks from today." I checked my watch. "Sheriff—I mean Tyler—the Inn's official grand opening is in an hour, right when dinner is served. I know this is a crime scene and all, but do you know when the crime scene will be processed?"

Tyler bit his bottom lip as he considered the situation. "Just keep your guests away from the garden for the next couple of hours. The coroner and crime scene techs should be done soon. I've already asked them to be discreet."

He rose. "One more thing. I will have more questions for you and your family after I debrief with the Shady Creek investigators. I'll need to speak with you, Pearl, and Ruby further since you were the ones who discovered the body. I'll call you later."

That gave me time to talk some sense into Aunt Pearl. That the sheriff hadn't kept her under watch told me that he didn't really consider her a suspect. Being Pearl, though, meant she was bound to say some incriminating things.

# CHAPTER 9

*A*fter dinner we steered our guests towards *The Witching Post* for after-dinner drinks. That would hopefully occupy them until darkness fell and the police finished up at the gazebo. The sooner the police finished their evidence gathering the better. I worried that guests might stroll around the grounds since there wasn't much to do in town after dark. It would be disastrous if they stumbled upon the murder scene.

It was seven p.m. by the time we had cleared the tables and washed the dishes. I walked outside and was relieved to see empty parking spaces where the coroner's van and the Shady Creek police vehicles had been parked earlier. Sheriff Gates' SUV was gone too, his parking spot now occupied by Brayden's shiny black BMW sedan.

I was relieved and angry at the same time. Brayden must have heard of the murder by now, yet he hadn't even called or tracked me down to see if I was okay. Even his part-time bartender duties rated higher than my safety and well-being.

My heart stopped as I glanced toward the garden and saw the yellow crime scene tape still draped around the gazebo. I made a mental note to call the sheriff to ask if the crime scene tape could be removed before morning.

In just one day it felt like my whole life had changed. We'd opened our Inn after months of hard work only to face the tragic murder of a guest and possible financial ruin. My wedding rehearsal had been absent the groom, and having to explain Brayden's absence to Sheriff Gates made me have second thoughts about our wedding and our relationship. Getting married shouldn't be second place to anything, yet that was how I felt in Brayden's world. I would never be first.

Then there was Tyler Gates. I was blindsided by my attraction to him. Aside from his looks, I felt a deeper chemistry, something I had never felt with Brayden. But that was stupid, since I didn't even know him.

I found myself hoping he would stick around for a while, and not just to maintain law and order. But so what if he did?

Aunt Pearl was right about one thing. Unless I cared enough to change things up, nothing would happen. She had meant using my magic, but it applied to every area of my life, including my love life. I was responsible for my own happiness, and it was up to me to change my life. I walked towards *The Witching Post*, lost in thought.

The bar had operated for several years, but didn't get a whole lot of business. Naturally I wanted to make sure our guests were enjoying themselves, but I also wanted to give Brayden a piece of my mind. Was I just an afterthought to him? The more I thought about it, the angrier I became.

The bar was housed in a separate building off the inn's circular driveway. I crossed the driveway and savored the cool night air. A light breeze blew in from the foothills and the creek gurgled a hundred feet away. Mother Nature was oblivious to the tragic events just a few hours ago.

The outdoors seemed to invigorate me with fresh perspective on Aunt Pearl's antics. She wasn't happy about interlopers in her town but she would eventually get over it. We just needed to somehow involve her more, in a way that didn't unduly distress our visitors. We could discreetly use our talents to help the sheriff solve Sebastien Plant's murder. As long as I kept Aunt Pearl in my sights, she couldn't make things worse.

She had seemed intrigued by the note; maybe she could help me decipher it. The note had stuck in my memory because it seemed like it had been written by a local, or at least someone who wanted to appear to be local. I felt a catch in my throat I remembered the verse. I saw it clearly in my mind, remembering how it described precisely Aunt Pearl's sentiments:

THOUGH YOU TRAVEL FAR and wide,
    You'd be best to run and hide,
    Your business was built on travel,
    But it is here that you become unravelled,

YOU HAVE no business staying here,
    Not to taste our food, nor drink our beer,

LEAVE WESTWICK CORNERS ALONE,
    And while you still can, go back home.

HANDS off our town and land
    If you do not,
    You will be caught
    And never ever walk this earth again.

THE THREAT SEEMED DIRECTED at Sebastien Plant, but as Aunt Pearl had noted earlier, there was no point in threatening someone already dead, assuming the murder was premeditated. Was the note meant to scare off Tonya Plant? If so, it pointed to someone opposed to development in Westwick Corners.

Except no one other than Aunt Pearl and me even knew about the Plants' secret development plans. I had seen the plans only after the murder. Presumably Aunt Pearl had too.

Maybe instead of a clue, the note was meant to sidetrack the investigation instead.

I stopped in my tracks as I visualized the note. I hadn't noticed before that Unraveled was spelled with two L's, either a British spelling or a mistake. Proof enough that the note was left by an outsider, a non-American, to deflect blame onto someone local, like Aunt Pearl. That same person had undoubtedly bloodied her wand. I had no proof though, and without it my theory just sounded far-fetched, like I was looking for ways to clear my aunt. But how could I get to the bottom of things unless Aunt Pearl cooperated?

I shook my head and walked towards the bar. Voices drifted outside and lifted my spirits. I hoped that The Westwick Corners Inn's grand opening would bring lots of extra business to *The Witching Post* Bar and Grill.

I wasn't disappointed. Not only was the bar bustling with activity, it was standing room only. A few locals had even made the trek up the hill to mingle. Officially they came to show their support for our new business venture, but in reality they were here to check out and gossip about the out-of-town guests.

There wasn't much going on in Westwick Corners at the best of times, but the locals seemed surprisingly unaware of the murder. I was thankful that Sheriff Gates and the Shady Creek police had been discreet. Other than the police, only Aunt Pearl, Mom, and I knew. I wanted to keep it that way, at least for tonight while the locals mingled with our paying guests.

I also wanted to break the story in *The Westwick Corners Weekly*. It wasn't often I had a scoop before the rumor mill. By tomorrow there would be more details and hopefully some leads. Any leak before then would just scare the guests away and ruin the Inn's reputation.

Since *The Witching Post* was one of only two local restaurants and the only bar in town, we usually got a decent crowd on the weekends. But tonight's action was more than I had ever seen, a full house. The receipts would probably pay our bills for a month or more.

I spotted Brayden behind the bar. Most locals needed several jobs to make ends meet and Brayden was no exception. He worked the bar on the weekends. I was relieved to see him busily filling drink orders, but disappointed that he took his part-time job more seriously than me. I was still furious at his earlier absence, but at least I didn't have to cover as bartender.

"Cen!" Brayden waved and flashed his brilliant white smile at me. "We need to talk."

We sure did, though I expected our topics would differ. "You were a no-show at your own wedding rehearsal, Brayden. How could you?"

"Aw, Cen, cut me some slack. Something big came up and I couldn't leave city hall." He shrugged. "It's no big deal, right? The real wedding rehearsal is in a few days." He turned and waved as two local farmers sat down at the opposite end of the bar.

"You think it's all a big joke, don't you?" My face flushed as I fought to keep my cool.

"Of course not." He reached an arm around me. "It's just that you and your mom tend to over-plan things."

"I over-plan?" Nothing ever happened otherwise, since Brayden never planned anything. I had to do everything. I probably over-compensated for Brayden's spontaneity since his plans never seemed to come to fruition. He was a dreamer, not a doer. "You don't do anything other than show up. Do you know how much work goes into planning a wedding?"

"Relax, Cen. I appreciate everything you do, but two rehearsals are a bit much. I just figured the pre-rehearsal wasn't that big of a deal."

"It was a very big deal. Our VIP guest, Sebastien Plant, was murdered in the gazebo. It would have helped if you were here a few hours earlier." At least we had discovered the body and not a guest.

"It's not like I could have prevented the murder, Cen. I heard all about it from Sheriff Gates. He arrived quickly, right?" Brayden placed a coaster and a wineglass of *Witching Hour Red* in front of me.

I stared at the glass, aware Brayden was trying to make amends. Normally he preferred that I drink non-alcoholic beverages now that he was mayor. I preferred wine. He was obviously trying to smooth things over to avoid a fight.

"Yes, but we could have used your help to manage the situation. A dead body isn't exactly great for our grand opening." I thought back to my encounter with Sheriff Tyler Gates and felt a flutter in my chest. His lean, muscular build and those melting brown eyes...

"Cen?"

"Huh?"

"I got here as soon as I could."

"You were over three hours late. Since when do city hall meetings extend till 7:30 p.m.?" I didn't wait for his answer. "And what was more important than a murder at your fiancée's place?"

He shrugged. "Rush hour traffic."

"What traffic? Everybody in town was already here. Except for you." Westwick Corners traffic was nonexistent, especially since Aunt Pearl's highway sign pyrotechnics made us invisible to passing motorists. Brayden's absence had only worsened my pre-wedding jitters and made me re-evaluate our relationship. For the first time I realized that, while Brayden loved me, I would always be a distant second to his plans and ambitions. He considered me more of a sidekick than an equal partner. I hadn't realized that until this very moment.

"Cen, c'mon. I can't just leave my job whenever your mom decides."

"But she asked us weeks ago. You promised you would be there." The wedding invitations had been sent, the menu prepared and the venue organized. Backing out or postponing the wedding would destroy Brayden. He was also hugely popular as mayor, so everyone in town would probably turn against me. On the other hand, I couldn't live a lie. How had a man I'd met less than twenty-four hours ago trigger such doubts about my future?

"I had a meeting in Shady Creek, okay? Traffic was bad on the highway, but I'm here now." He grinned and turned to fill two pint-glasses. "Being mayor isn't just a nine-to-five job, Cen. I got here as soon as I could."

"Fine." My job wasn't nine-to-five either, but I didn't use it as an excuse. It was just like Brayden to gloss over my feelings, and imply that somehow things were my fault, and that his job was more important than mine.

Brayden was the only guy I'd ever even dated, but I felt like I didn't really even know him anymore. I had always assumed Brayden and I were meant to be together and never thought much about other men before.

Correction. Of course I thought about them. Sometimes I was even attracted to them. But this was more than a physical attraction. I was drawn to Tyler Gates in a way I'd never experienced before. I couldn't put my finger on what it was, but it was there.

Like all the sheriffs before him, Tyler Gates was obviously damaged goods or he would have found a better-paying job in a larger town. I found him interesting simply because there was something missing between Brayden and me.

Here I was, about to make the biggest mistake of my life over a man I didn't even know. Other than Brayden, Tyler Gates was the only man in town not collecting Social Security. He just looked good because everything about Brayden suddenly seemed all wrong.

"You should have been here earlier. I'm tired of being taken for granted."

Brayden ran a hand through his perfectly styled hair. "Public service involves personal sacrifices, Cen. Work comes first. We discussed all this when I ran for mayor."

I didn't remember discussing anything of the sort. "What, exactly, is more important than me?"

Brayden threw his hands up in exasperation. "It's just not that simple, Cen. You know I can't discuss confidential city business with you."

Aside from Brayden's girlfriend, I was also the press. Brayden was right that nothing stayed secret in Westwick Corners for long. "Does work come before our wedding? Will you be a no-show for that too?"

Brayden rolled his eyes. "Of course not, but I have to make tough choices sometimes."

"A murder and you can't even show up?"

"You can't expect that I would know that." He placed the two pints of frosty pale ale in front of the two silver-haired farmers. Then he turned back to me.

"You said earlier that the sheriff told you right away." What could possibly be more important than a murder on the sheriff's first day on the job? Something in Brayden's priorities trumped murder.

There was a first time for everything.

I hadn't given marrying Brayden a second thought until this afternoon and now I wondered if my head was screwed on straight. "We didn't discuss anything. You decided what you wanted, just like you always do. For once I'd like to have been part of what you wanted." My voice rose above the music and heads turned in my direction.

"We'll talk about it later." Brayden dropped his gaze and focused on mixing a martini.

I fumed inside. Brayden had been elected mayor only a few

months ago, so I should cut him some slack. On the other hand, mayor had always been a part-time job.

Westwick Corners had less than a thousand people, but Brayden had adopted his new role with gusto because he saw it as a stepping stone to greater things. Being mayor opened doors and allowed him to hob nob with state and federal politicians.

But I wasn't about to be dismissed by him. He needed to answer to his constituents, including me. "No, I want to talk now."

But Brayden was already out of earshot, down at the opposite end of the bar replenishing drinks.

Aunt Pearl was right. Brayden really did take me for granted, and I was tired of it. We had known each other practically all our lives, yet I never felt less connected to him. His political ambitions trumped our relationship, and even the needs of our little town that he was supposed to represent.

I placed my half-full wineglass on the bar and stood. The bar was standing room only, and half a dozen guests danced to the beat of the country-rock music that pumped through the speakers.

My thoughts turned back to Plant's murder and my story. It occurred to me that it was almost impossible to objectively report a crime that occurred on our property. Maybe it was a hint of things to come, since any sort of journalistic independence was also impossible once I married the mayor.

Great.

I would have to give up the newspaper and my job.

The last thing I wanted to become was a political wife, supporting my husband with no life of my own. Did I really love Brayden, or was I just comfortable with him? I had gotten so swept up in other people's expectations that I didn't know the answer.

My attraction to Tyler Gates was nothing more than a physical one. But it was a pull I had never felt towards Brayden, and I liked the way it felt. I wanted to feel it again.

Whatever the feeling was or wasn't, I needed to stop and figure things out. I would disappoint everyone, but I had already wasted too much time trying to please everyone else except myself. I stood and moved towards Brayden at the end of the bar. He had finished with the drinks and was wiping the bar.

I took a deep breath. "About the wedding, I—"

He kissed me on the cheek. "You read my mind. Do we have room on the guest list for the governor and his wife? It's a great opportunity to get to know them better."

That just confirmed my suspicions that my dreams would always take a back seat to Brayden's social climbing and political ambitions. I would have to curtail my magic. Witches are the worst baggage for political careers, and Brayden's aspirations were much bigger than Westwick Corners. He planned to be state governor one day.

No stories, no magic, no love.

No future together. Why had it taken me so long to see it?

"No." I had no time for a debate. I had to get working at the Inn.

"What do you mean, no? We can't make room for two more people?"

I sighed. Brayden always saw things from his point of view—not our point of view. I would hold off until morning before I told him the wedding was off.

"Not now." I glimpsed Aunt Pearl from the corner of my eye. She wore her ancient 1970's gray Adidas tracksuit, the one reserved for athletic endeavors. I ignored Brayden's objections and followed her outdoors. She was headed for the gazebo and, no doubt, trouble.

"Aunt Pearl, Mom needs you inside."

My aunt turned and stared at me. She narrowed her eyes and said something I couldn't quite hear. "Can you repeat that?"

She scowled and changed direction. I trailed behind her towards the Inn's front steps. I felt a tug at my arm and turned to see Brayden at my side. I was alarmed that he had followed me outside. That meant no one was tending bar.

"What's gotten into you lately?" He grabbed my other arm and we locked eyes. "You're not the same."

"I haven't changed, but you have. If you don't have time for me now, what happens when we get married?" I broke from his embrace and scanned the garden for my aunt. She had disappeared from view.

"It's not that, it's just that things are busy right now and—"

"No more excuses, Brayden." I turned towards the garden.

"Cen, c'mon." Brayden stood motionless with his arms crossed. Waiting for me to come to him.

"We'll talk tomorrow." I had half-hoped he would follow me, but it was probably better that he didn't. I wasn't sure how and when to say it, but suddenly everything was crystal clear. I wasn't marrying Brayden Banks.

And he wasn't going to like it one bit.

# CHAPTER 10

*I* followed Aunt Pearl across the lawn and driveway into the rose garden. Just as I feared, she made a beeline for the gazebo. I shuddered. Her plans almost certainly involved repelling tourists, but she was about to further incriminate herself in the process. A crime scene on our property was horrific enough, but a compromised crime scene was much worse. Especially one compromised by a witch.

"Aunt Pearl, wait!" Her pace was far faster than a normal seventy-year-old body could muster, so I knew magic was involved. Even in the dim twilight I saw the gasoline canister in her hand. I broke into a sprint and closed the gap just steps from the yellow crime scene tape. "Put the can down."

"Make me." She smirked, set down the canister, and rolled up her tracksuit sleeves.

I had no choice but to counter with some magic of my own. We were two feet from the gazebo steps and a millisecond from disaster.

Whether it was luck or instinct, I wasn't sure, but I stopped her in her tracks and disintegrated the gasoline jerry can.

Aunt Pearl gasped.

We stared silently at the residual poof of smoke.

Disaster averted, at least for the moment. "You can't destroy a crime scene, Aunt Pearl. It's also too late to destroy anything. The police have already gathered the evidence."

She swirled around and faced me. "And you can't go around destroying other people's things, Cendrine." She stared down at her empty hands. No trace remained of the gasoline canister.

"You left me with no choice." My heart pounded in my chest. I waited for her to counter with another vengeful act, this time directed at me.

Instead she smiled. "Not bad, considering how little you practice. You really can work magic when you put your mind to it."

For once my talents felt more like a blessing than a curse. I couldn't help but feel a little proud despite the circumstances. Aunt Pearl rarely gave compliments, especially when it came to magic.

I avoided spells because magic felt like cheating to me. I thought it gave me an unfair advantage and I was strongly opposed to conjuring my way out of trouble. I had resorted to Aunt Pearl's bag of tricks, but at least I wasn't destroying a crime scene. "Only out of necessity. Let's go back to the house."

Aunt Pearl ignored my request and turned back to the gazebo. "You just need to apply yourself better, Cen. Why not start here?" My serial arsonist aunt snapped her fingers and a flaming stick materialized in her hand.

I snapped my fingers and conjured up a bucket of water, but it was too little too late. I threw the bucket in her direction, but she had already reached the gazebo stairs. I tackled her and we rolled off the steps and into the grass. We stopped just inches from the crime scene tape.

"You tricked me!" I rolled off her and sat up only to see Tyler Gates.

"What the hell's going on here?" The sheriff stamped out the fire with his boot. His smirk vanished when he recognized Pearl.

That was exactly the question I had been about to ask my aunt. Why was she hell bent on destroying the gazebo? Was she somehow involved?

"Thank goodness you're here, Sheriff." Aunt Pearl sniffed. "She attacked without warning."

The corners of Tyler Gates' mouth turned up ever so slightly. "Is that right?"

"She provoked me." As the words tumbled out, I realized we sounded like a couple of bickering school kids.

Embarrassing.

"She's trouble." Aunt Pearl pointed an accusing finger at me.

I rolled my eyes and brushed grass and dirt off my clothes as I stood.

"I'd be careful if I were you," he said. "The gazebo's still off limits and I haven't cleared either of you as suspects yet."

I assumed his comment was for Aunt Pearl's benefit, since he had already checked my alibi. I had been at the newspaper all morning, confirmed by my building's security cameras and a couple of other early risers in the building. I hadn't left the office until I drove home at three p.m. and headed straight to the gazebo.

Aunt Pearl's whereabouts were unaccounted for from nine a.m. until just before noon, when she had arrived at my office after the highway fire fiasco. She claimed to have gone directly to the Inn after leaving my office. Mom could easily verify Aunt Pearl's claim of readying the guest rooms prior to her highway arson. I knew my aunt well enough not to accept her statements at face value, but in my heart I also knew that she wasn't a killer. But the law operated on cold, hard facts, not sentimental feelings.

Aunt Pearl grabbed the railing and pulled herself upright to all of her five feet zero and scowled at the sheriff. "You'll never figure it out on your own. If you ask nicely enough, I just might help you."

"Start by telling me where you were this morning." Sheriff Gates crossed his arms.

"As if you didn't know already." Aunt Pearl sneered.

"She's right," I said. "Wasn't she burning down the highway sign?"

"That was in the morning. The afternoon is still unaccounted for," Tyler said. "I need a complete accounting of your whereabouts, Pearl. Some cooperation would be nice."

Cooperation from Aunt Pearl was like a getting a cash advance from the Mafia. You'd get what you asked for, but you'd pay dearly.

Aunt Pearl snorted. "Let's see...I went to the gas station around eleven. I guess you know what happened after that."

Tyler pulled out his pad. "Do you have a receipt for the gas? That would establish the time."

"My word's not good enough?"

I knew without a doubt that Aunt Pearl hadn't bought the gasoline; she had conjured it out of thin air. She couldn't admit that to the sheriff though. I grew increasingly worried about her evasiveness and lack of an alibi.

Tyler ignored her question and countered with one of his own. "Where were you before the gas station?"

"I'll tell you if you cancel my fine." Aunt Pearl crossed her arms and snorted.

"Not a chance. The ticket's already issued, so I couldn't change it even if I wanted to. You'll have to fight it in court."

"You had your chance, Sheriff," Pearl said. "Life in this town can be easy or hard. Choose your medicine."

"Aunt Pearl!" I clamped a hand on my aunt's shoulder. The last thing we needed was a standoff with the law. "Answer the sheriff's question so we can leave and let him get back to work."

Aunt Pearl hovered a few inches from the crime scene tape, but she didn't cross over. She glared at Sheriff Gates. "I was working at the Inn with Ruby until I went to the gas station. This is just turning into a witch hunt." Pearl crossed her arms. "Can I go now?"

I glared at my aunt. Her thinly veiled witch references got on my nerves. Of course that was exactly her intention.

Tyler Gates nodded. "I'll verify your alibi with Ruby, of course."

The sheriff nodded. "Don't even think about leaving town. I'll be watching you." He pointed two fingers at his eyes, then Pearl's.

"Go ahead." Pearl brushed my hand off her shoulder and stormed off towards the Inn.

At least our new sheriff had a sense of humor. Aunt Pearl wouldn't leave town; she just wished everybody else would. At any rate, the sheriff's words had their intended effect. Pearl inched back across the garden towards the house in an exaggerated arthritic gait. I glanced back at the gazebo. "Is the uh, body gone yet?"

"The coroner took him away an hour ago." Tyler shone his light into the gazebo.

I felt his eyes on me as I turned to the gazebo. With the body now gone, the only evidence of the terrible deed were bloodstains on the wooden floor. I gasped as I saw Aunt Pearl's wand propped up by the entrance, bagged as evidence. Had she known it was still in the gazebo when she tried to set it on fire? There was something she wasn't telling me, and I didn't like it one bit.

# CHAPTER 11

*I*t was after nine p.m. and darkness had fallen by the time I returned to the Inn. The last few hours had been a flurry of activity between the murder investigation, keeping tabs on Aunt Pearl, and ensuring things stayed on track with our hotel guests.

I hadn't talked to Mom for a while and was anxious to see how she was making out. I found her in the kitchen washing dishes. She always washed dishes by hand even though we had a commercial grade dishwasher. Heck, as a witch, she could even use a spell to wash them and complete her "to-do" list in a split second. But the perfectionist in her insisted on doing things the hard way. By the time she checked and rechecked her spells, it was just as quick to do things the manual, mortal way. Mom and I were exactly the same in that respect. We were insecure about our natural talents. Magic seemed an unfair advantage sometimes.

"Oh Cen, I can't believe we've got a murder on our hands." Her eyes were bloodshot and swollen, like she'd been crying. Her clothes were disheveled and her apron was on sideways, completely out of character from her normally immaculate appearance. "What are the odds of this happening on our grand opening?"

"Pretty good, if you think about it. The perfect time to hit tourism is before it even gets off the ground."

"I can't imagine anyone in town going to that extreme. Who would kill to stop progress?" Mom brushed her hands on her apron. "That note scares me."

I recounted my suspicions about the note writer and the curious spelling of unraveled. "Aunt Pearl doesn't use British spelling. Whoever wrote the note obviously wanted it to sound like it came from her, though."

"Don't be ridiculous, Cen. Pearl would never harm anyone. How could you even suggest that?"

"I think that's probably how things appear to the sheriff. A lot of the evidence seems to point to Aunt Pearl, and the sheriff has to investigate all leads. I know she didn't do it, but there's definitely something she isn't telling us." I grabbed a dishtowel and tackled the dishes in the drying rack. "She always carries her wand. Why didn't she take it from the gazebo? I've never known her to leave it anywhere unattended. She could have grabbed it before the sheriff arrived, but she didn't."

Mom shrugged. "She either forgot, or didn't want to disrupt the crime scene."

"Since when does she not want to disrupt things? According to her, it wasn't part of the crime scene. She said she dropped it when she fell on top of me."

Mom frowned but didn't say anything.

"Did she have her wand when you two walked over to the gazebo?"

"I don't remember. I was so preoccupied with getting things ready for the Inn's grand opening that I didn't notice." Mom dropped the pot she was washing. It fell into the sink with a metallic clang.

I felt a twinge of guilt that I hadn't been at the Inn to help.

"There's been so much to do here, it's overwhelming. Pearl was gone all morning, so I had to do everything myself."

Now I was the one in shock. "Wait a sec—Aunt Pearl told the sheriff she was here with you until eleven and said you would vouch for her."

Mom sighed and raised a hand to her forehead. "I'm not going to lie for her. She went out early this morning, and I didn't see her again until the afternoon. What has she got us into?"

"I don't know, but unless she tells us where and what she's been doing, we can't help her. I'm pretty sure Sheriff Gates thinks she's guilty of something." I hated to think of Aunt Pearl being wrongly accused. For a reason I couldn't quite explain, I also wanted to make a good impression on Tyler Gates. "Whatever she's hiding can't be as bad as murder."

"She's pretty stubborn, Cen." Mom shook her head. "The world could come crashing down around her and she would still keep her secrets. She creates a lot of trouble for herself that way."

"Well, if she wants her wand back, she'll have to explain things. The sheriff has collected it as evidence. He thinks it's her cane though."

Mom's mouth dropped open. "Pearl's an actual suspect?"

"He didn't say that exactly, but her dislike of tourism gives her a motive, and that note sounds like her to a tee. Add in her wand at the crime scene and she's a natural suspect. I'm sure the sheriff sees that."

"But we were at the gazebo too," Mom protested. "Why aren't we suspects?"

"I've got an alibi. I was working all day until three p.m. The investigators can probably estimate a time of death by the condition of the body." I shuddered as I recalled falling onto Plant's corpse.

"And I was in town most of the morning, getting last minute things for dinner. Lots of people saw me. I even ran into the sheriff," Mom said.

"You see? Aunt Pearl lied because she has no alibi." A lie or a lie of omission?

"Maybe she got her times mixed up?" Mom's expression indicated her disbelief even as she uttered the words.

"We both know that's impossible. She's way too sharp for that."

"True." Mom nodded. "But she probably thinks her whereabouts are none of the sheriff's business. She gets kind of ornery when people keep tabs on her."

"That's fine most of the time, but not now when there's a murder. Everything points to her, except for one thing," I said. "The killer knew his victim."

"Oh?" Mom plunged her hands into the soapy water. "The sheriff tell you that?"

I shook my head. "Attacking a victim's face implies a personal relationship. Whether it's bludgeoning them to death or covering their face after the fact. Sebastien Plant knew his killer. As far as I know, he's never met Aunt Pearl." The television show *Forensic Files* had taught me to look for clues hiding in plain sight, and Plant's head and facial injuries spoke volumes.

"You watch too many crime shows, Cen."

"Maybe, but it's the only lead we have right now. It's an important clue. Whoever did this has to be caught."

Mom pulled her hands out of the dishpan and threw them up in the air, splashing sudsy water everywhere. "Pearl is a lot of things, but she's not a killer. But I agree she's hiding something. I just don't think I'll be able to pry her secrets out of her. She won't talk."

"She has to," I said. "Unless she comes clean and explains everything, she could get charged with murder." Aunt Pearl wasn't one to stay silent about much of anything. A simple explanation would clear her as a suspect, yet she wouldn't provide one.

Her silence also spelled the death knell for the entire town since tourists wouldn't visit as long as a killer walked among us. But Westwick Corners had eked out an existence for well over a hundred years. Come hell or high water, it would last another century if I had anything to do with it.

# CHAPTER 12

*W*hatever Aunt Pearl did or didn't admit to, it didn't explain the blood on her wand. Someone had either stolen her wand and used it, or she had used it herself. I visualized the wand in my mind. The blood on the tip was already dry. It had been a hot day but the gazebo was shady. The blood would have taken fifteen minutes or longer to dry.

I shuddered as I remembered the stiffness of Plant's body as I fell on top of him. I was certain he was dead a lot longer than fifteen minutes. More like hours earlier.

"Aunt Pearl's wand has no value to anyone else. Why would anyone steal it in the first place?"

"It has value to another witch." Mom placed the last of the plates in the drying rack and drained the water from the sink.

That hadn't occurred to me. "But only Pearl can unlock her wand." Modern wands were hi-tech and Pearl's was especially so. It required a combination of her fingerprint and a password. Even magic used biometrics nowadays.

"A witch doesn't have to unlock it and use it," Mom said. "She just

71

has to keep the wand away from Pearl. Pearl becomes powerless, unable to cast magic spells without her wand."

"Why would someone want to stop her magic?" I flashed back to Aunt Pearl's flaming stick at the gazebo. She had conjured that up, so she still wasn't being truthful. There was still something she wasn't telling us, and that wasn't good.

"I have no idea, but I can't imagine why anyone other than a witch would steal and sabotage her wand." Mom wiped her brow. "Whoever did this wants to make Pearl a scapegoat, but who?"

"Someone who wants to get away with murder. Aunt Pearl goes to jail and the murderer gets off scot-free." My list of Pearl-haters included half the town, but I didn't dare voice my fears. Mom was blind to both her sister's faults and her long list of enemies. Most were town locals though, ordinary mortals without special powers. None were cold-blooded killers.

"The killer puts away two people." Mom frowned. "I still think it's another witch, though."

"We're the only witches in town," I said. "Maybe we should make a list of who might want to hurt Aunt Pearl."

"Hazel and Pearl are fighting," Mom said.

"You don't think—"

"No, even Witch Hazel wouldn't go that far." Mom untied her apron and tossed it on the counter. "But if the killer is another witch, Pearl is in big trouble. She'll never be able to explain every-thing and clear her name."

Of course.

Witches could easily alter clues, even forensic evidence. Aunt Pearl wasn't the only one who needed help. Sheriff Gates did too. If he expected his stint in Westwick Corners to be a slack post in a sleepy little town, he was in for a supernatural surprise. I had no choice but to at least investigate the Witch Hazel angle that our sheriff was unaware of. "Can we somehow find out about Hazel's whereabouts?"

Hazel Black was Pearl's best friend until their major falling out a year ago. Aside from being an accomplished witch, she was also the president of Witches International Community Craft Association or WICCA, the worldwide governing body for witches.

I couldn't fathom Hazel going as far as to kill an innocent man and pin it on Aunt Pearl. On the other hand, Hazel had cursed my brother Alan and turned him into a Border collie. I never saw that one coming either.

Mom's brows knitted together. "I suppose we could ask Amber."

Aunt Amber was WICCA's vice-president and saw Hazel all the time. If she vouched for Hazel's whereabouts, we could quickly eliminate her as a suspect. Aunt Pearl wouldn't want her sister Amber involved, but we didn't have much choice. "What if she tells Hazel? She might wonder why we're asking."

"At this point, I think we have to." Mom dried her hands and snapped her fingers.

A holographic image slowly solidified in front of us. Aunt Amber smoothed her ginger hair and tucked a lock behind her ear. She looked as gorgeous and polished as ever, but distracted, like we had interrupted her.

"This better be good. You caught me right in the middle of a spell." Amber, like Hazel, lived in London, England. Westwick Corners simply couldn't contain her.

"Sorry. It's kind of important," Mom said.

"It's barely after six a.m. here, Ruby. You know I'm not a morning person. This better be good."

It was still Friday night here, but London was nine hours ahead. The sheriff's timeline would be confirmed by the coroner, but the murder had likely occurred sometime between noon and three p.m., when we had discovered the body. That was between nine p.m. and midnight London time.

"I'm afraid it's not good at all." I quickly recapped the day's events, the murder, and the incriminating evidence that pointed to Pearl. "Pearl and Hazel are still feuding. Maybe Hazel set her up and planted her wand at the crime scene?"

73

As a witch, Hazel could travel here and back to London in less than an hour. In the absence of other leads, it was up to us to rule out any supernatural suspects. They would never come to light in Sheriff Gates' investigation.

"I wouldn't put revenge past Witch Hazel," Aunt Amber said. "But I can't see her killing an innocent stranger to frame Pearl."

"We aren't blaming Hazel, but we can't rule her out either," I said. "Do you know where she was last night?"

Aunt Amber shrugged and held up her palms. "Sleeping like everyone else, I assume, Cen. I haven't seen her since she left work on Friday, and I won't see her again until Monday morning at the office. I don't keep tabs on her outside of work."

"Anyone other than Penny who can account for her where-abouts?" Penny Black was Hazel's daughter. Penny was also Alan's ex-girlfriend and the reason behind Hazel's Border collie curse. Hazel Black lived alone. Pearl was—or at least had been—Hazel's only close friend.

"Have you tried her boyfriend?" Aunt Amber brought a magenta-hued nail to her lips adorned in a matching shade. "He'll probably have an idea."

"Witch Hazel has a boyfriend?" I couldn't imagine anyone wanting to hook up with Hazel. Aside from her domineering personality, she was all business. In addition to her role as WICCA president, she was a shrewd entrepreneur.

"Surprised me too. They've been seeing each other for a couple of months. I'm trying to remember his name. Seb somebody?"

"Sebastien Plant?"

Mom's mouth dropped open and she looked as if she was about to keel over.

"That's the name. You know him?" Aunt Amber's image wavered. "I've got to go—my herbs are burning!"

"Wait!" But it was too late. Aunt Amber was gone.

I turned to Mom. "Sebastien Plant's killer left a note with British spelling. Hazel is British. Do you think she did it?"

Mom shook her head emphatically. "Neither Hazel nor Pearl are capable of anything like this, Cen. We'd better talk to both of them right away."

Sebastien Plant's bloodied face flashed in my mind. Both Hazel and Tonya knew him intimately, but only Hazel was British.

While Hazel and Pearl weren't speaking to each other, they had been best friends for decades. Was it possible that Pearl was covering for her friend?

# CHAPTER 13

*A*unt Amber's information didn't shed any new light on things other than the bombshell about Hazel's affair with Sebastien Plant. Nor did it solve our immediate problem.

Pearl was AWOL again. I had to track her down because there was no telling what she might do to get her wand back. Mom was already close to a nervous breakdown and Pearl could easily push her over the edge.

"You've got to keep tabs on her, Cen. I can't leave the Inn, and I'm worried that she's about to do something crazy. We've all got so much invested in the Inn's success. Pearl can ruin things in an instant."

This time Mom wasn't overreacting. "I'll find her." I headed out the front doors and across the driveway to *The Witching Post*. The last person I wanted to see right now was Brayden, but he was probably too busy bartending to notice me anyway.

I would check the bar for Aunt Pearl and then make a quick exit. As I pulled open the front door, I almost collided with a buxom blonde in a shimmering gold lamé evening gown. Her vintage gown seemed out of place yet strangely familiar.

I only saw the back of her low cut dress, but I recognized Aunt Pearl's talisman bracelet as it jangled when she brushed past me. Carolyn Conroe, Aunt Pearl's Marilyn Monroe alter ego, headed straight for the bar.

My heart sank. The hours were ticking away, yet I couldn't talk to Aunt Pearl about Sebastien Plant and Hazel until she changed back to her normal form. That could take a while, depending on how much trouble she got herself into.

"Where can I get a cocktail in this joint?" Carolyn's voice rose above the din and suddenly all conversation ceased.

Brayden gave her a dismissive wave. "Can you wait? Happy Hour starts in fifteen minutes."

Brayden never got the concept behind Happy Hour. Instead of enticing customers early in the evening, he basically gave whoever waited long enough a half-price discount. All the locals took advantage of his weird timing and never bothered to show up until later on.

The only upside to Brayden's strange promotion was that Carolyn didn't yet have a drink in her hand. He also knew of Aunt Pearl's alter ego, though he believed that Carolyn Conroe stemmed from a personality disorder and too much makeup. Aunt Pearl's magic was that good. Unfortunately her outcomes were never good, so I just hoped Brayden had enough sense to water down her drinks. A drunk Carolyn was much, much worse than a sober Pearl. There was no telling what she might do.

Carolyn threw her head back in a throaty laugh. "I'll be back for you, lover."

Brayden's face flushed. Pearl had just embarrassed him as a form of revenge.

Everyone stared in our direction just as a gust of wind from who knew where blew Carolyn's skirt hem upwards. A mischievous grin spread across her face. She slowly patted down her skirt, but not before giving a peep show to just about every red-blooded male in Westwick Corners.

A crowd gathered around Carolyn. She clearly enjoyed every second of her time in the spotlight.

I ignored the wolf whistles and scanned the bar. The bar stools were full, with guests interspersed among the locals. I noted with satisfaction that almost all the guests were present. As long as they remained in the bar, they wouldn't notice the yellow crime scene tape that still surrounded the gazebo.

I spotted Tonya Plant alone at a corner table. She was almost as well-known as Sebastien. They made such an odd couple though. Tonya was in her early thirties, at least twenty years younger than Sebastien. She seemed tiny compared to her morbidly obese husband and even smaller in person. She wore her fine blonde hair in a pixie cut and dressed like a royal in a couture dress with tiny embroidered rosettes. She tapped a kitten heel absent-mindedly as she nursed a glass of red wine. She stared open-mouthed at Carolyn's antics.

Carolyn noticed immediately and made a beeline for Tonya's table.

Great.

I glanced towards the entrance a few feet away where Mom stood just inside the doorway. She had somehow gotten wind of Pearl's plans. One look at her face told me how worried she was.

I walked back towards her and took her aside. "We've got to neutralize Aunt Pearl." She was already a murder suspect, and now she was spoiling for a fight. Now wasn't the time for Carolyn's attention-getting antics. "Can't you talk some sense into her?"

Mom shook her head. "She won't listen to me. At least being here means she's not snooping around the guests' rooms." The house-keeping job was meant to keep her busy and out of trouble, and it wasn't hard since she could use her magic to automate tasks. Our idea backfired once she snooped in Tonya's room. I thought back to the development plans and feared the worst.

Mom tugged on my arm. "Do you think Pearl knows about Sebastien and Hazel?"

"I don't know. Hazel and Pearl haven't spoken to each other for a couple of months now. If she knows of Sebastien and didn't mention it to the sheriff, she looks even more suspicious." If I didn't know Aunt Pearl I would suspect her too. Everything she did seemed suspicious. Aunt Pearl liked to create a stir. If she knew of Hazel and Sebastien's affair, I had no doubt Tonya would discover it soon enough, if she didn't know already.

We tracked Carolyn with our eyes as she slinked across the dance floor towards Tonya's table. My pulse quickened as I updated Mom on Pearl's arson attempt at the gazebo. "It seems weird that she went to the gazebo to retrieve her wand. If someone stole it, how did she even know it was there in the first place? She must have known it would be confiscated as evidence."

A light bulb suddenly went off in my head. Aunt Pearl's Carolyn Conroe act was also magic, and much harder to pull off than her flaming stick at the gazebo. "How can Aunt Pearl do magic with no wand?"

"She's using something," Mom's face darkened. "What, I don't know yet. I just wish she'd stop and think about the rest of us sometimes. I've got to get back to the inn. Keep an eye on her, Cen."

Mom left and Carolyn sat down alone a few tables away from Tonya.

I was so deep in thought that I had walked up to the bar without even realizing it.

"The usual?" Brayden winked and placed a cranberry soda on a coaster in front of me.

I would have preferred a stiff drink, but I supposed we were back to the usual. Appearances could make or break a political career, and as his wife-to-be, anything I did reflected on him. At least that was how Brayden saw things.

I sipped my soda while he attended to other customers. Given the circumstances, maybe his choice of drink was better. Even an eyedropper of alcohol seriously lowered my inhibitions and willpower when it came to Brayden. Alcohol also interfered with my powers, and a quick scan of the room told me I might need magic to intervene with my aunt. Aunt Pearl—aka Carolyn—had again vacated her seat and now sat on the corner of Tonya's table. She belted out *Diamonds are a Girl's Best Friend* in a deep, throaty voice. She tilted her head back, diva-like.

Carolyn leaned further back until her hair dangled above Tonya's drink. Tonya pulled her chair back as Carolyn reclined even more. She winked seductively at her male admirers just as her hand slipped off the table. She lost her balance and rolled off, directly onto Tonya Plant's lap.

Tonya screamed.

I leapt from my bar stool and jumped between the two women faster than you can say "some like it hot".

I pulled Carolyn upright and off Tonya. Tonya's mouth dropped open in shock. She wore an angry expression and her designer dress wore a glass of wine. "What the hell are you doing?"

I scowled at my aunt before turning back to Tonya Plant. I pointedly ignored the red stain spreading across her pale yellow dress. Thankfully she was so busy cursing Carolyn that she hadn't noticed it yet. That gave me the opportunity to undo it. One chance with a spell that I hadn't practiced in years.

*One, two, three, make it not to be...*

I snapped my fingers, held my breath and hoped for the best.

I had rewound time back ten minutes earlier. At least that's what I had aimed for with my rusty magic. It seemed to work, since there was no red wine stain, no upturned table, and no Carolyn. We were back in time, a minute or so before things had deteriorated.

Now I just had to make things right. I snapped my fingers twice and cast a friendship spell.

It worked.

The two women were suddenly fast friends instead of adversaries. Carolyn Conroe sang *River of No Return* and leaned against Tonya's table.

"Bravo," Tonya giggled, clearly delighted at being noticed. The only red tone on her yellow dress were the pale pink rosettes. Tonya sipped her wine and enjoyed Carolyn's serenade.

Carolyn raised her arms and held the final note.

The bar fell silent for a few seconds until Tonya clapped. Carolyn bowed and the other patrons joined in the applause. Carolyn blew them a kiss and bowed.

I was very pleased with my alternate ending, though Carolyn clearly was not. She flipped me the finger and glared from across the room.

I smiled and waved. It was one of those rare times that I wished I had practiced my spells more. If I had, Aunt Pearl would have also remained unaware of my actions. Nevertheless, there wasn't much she could do about it now.

Exhausted, I returned to my seat at the bar. The spells had zapped what little energy I had left.

# CHAPTER 14

"You need a real drink." Brayden watched both of us as he placed a bottle of red wine and a glass on the bar. It was a bottle of *Witching Hour Red*, our finest vintage. He poured a glass and set it in front of me. "Just pretend she's not here."

I stared at my glassful of alcohol, momentarily alarmed that my rewind spell had impacted Brayden to the extent that he had forgotten he was mayor. I studied him for a moment before concluding that it wasn't about that at all. He was instead worried that I was about to cause a scene with Carolyn. Alcohol would incapacitate me.

So be it.

I downed half the glass. "I can't ignore her. I'm worried about what she might do next."

Brayden knew we were witches—at least sort of. He thought it was just a weird part of our family ancestry. Oh, he was vaguely aware of Aunt Pearl's Charm School and Mom's herbal potions, but he didn't take that stuff seriously. He equated it to things like astrology and palm reading. He just thought we shared weird hobbies. Regardless, we were always careful not to do our magic in front of him.

He was completely oblivious to the fact that I had just rewound his life by a few minutes. Too bad he couldn't completely forget our engagement. I agonized over how to break the news, especially since he was at this moment being very sweet to me.

"I'll keep an eye on Pearl. Just relax, Cen."

Few men marry into a family of witches easily, and on some level Brayden knew what he was getting into. I could never explain my situation to anyone who hadn't grown up with us in Westwick Corners. It just made sense for us to marry. The logic of it depressed me. Just because it was easy to marry him didn't mean that I should.

I sipped my wine, plagued by guilt over the oblivious souls in the bar who remained unaware that I had erased the last few minutes of their lives and replaced them with an alternate version. If only I could turn the clock back and prevent Plant's murder. It was too late for that. The most I could do was help Sheriff Gates track down the killer and see justice served.

Aunt Pearl, or rather Carolyn, followed me to the bar. She swore under her breath as she lifted her wineglass. "You complain about my magic." She tottered on her stilettos, threatening a second wine spill. "You're over the top, Cendrine West."

For a split-second I felt like a scolded five-year-old. Then I regained my senses.

"Go change, Aunt Pearl." I used my magic only as a last resort, but if any occasion warranted it, this one did. The whole town's future rested upon Aunt Pearl's civility. But I had to be careful, since undoing another witch's magic invited all sorts of trouble, even if she was my aunt.

Especially a witch much more powerful than I.

"Sssh." She held a finger to her lips. "You'll blow my cover."

"Are you drunk?" It was hard to tell if her unsteadiness was caused by her four-inch heels or too much alcohol.

She ignored me.

"Like my new dress, Cen? I just got it." Aunt Pearl shook her head as she hiked her dress high up her thigh, exposing skin. She balanced precariously on the stool. Her full wineglass tilted dangerously, threatening a second spill.

"I don't mean just a wardrobe change. Ditch the Carolyn act."

"But I was just getting started." Aunt Pearl pouted. "She's one of my favorites."

"Please, Aunt Pearl. We need to talk. You realize you're the only suspect in Sebastien Plant's murder?"

"You're accusing me of murder?" Aunt Pearl slammed her wineglass down on the bar, sending wine all over the bar.

"Of course not." I wiped wine droplets off my face. "But all the evidence points to you and no one else. I also need to talk to you about Hazel."

"What about Hazel?" She eyed me suspiciously.

"Not here." I was afraid to even bring up Hazel and Sebastien's supposed affair, but I had nowhere else to turn. It invited disaster, since Aunt Pearl didn't keep secrets very well. "We need somewhere private to talk."

She immediately brightened. "Let's go to Pearl's Charm School. But only if you agree to take my magic course."

"You'll change out of that ridiculous outfit and return to normal?" At least as close to normal as Aunt Pearl could get.

My aunt nodded. "I want my wand back, too."

"First things first." I couldn't do much to get her wand back, but I wasn't about to tell her that. My immediate priority was to neutralize Aunt Pearl before she did further damage. "I'll enroll at your stupid magic school, but only if you promise to stop your tricks for the rest of the weekend."

Her expression brightened immediately. "You will?"

"Yes." I regretted my promise already. "But only if you get our grand opening back on track and answer the sheriff's questions about the murder." Pearl's Charm School specialized in charms and

84

spells, two areas I was woefully deficient in. I had no desire to improve, but I was willing to do whatever I needed to placate Aunt Pearl and stop the carnage. "I'll meet you at Pearl's Charm School in half an hour."

I had barely finished my sentence when Aunt Pearl made a beeline for the exit and was gone. I scanned the bar and noted with satisfaction that the bar patrons had resumed playing pool, darts or whatever it was they had been doing before the Carolyn Conroe side show. Some of the locals had even left. *The Witching Post* slowly returned to its normal half-empty self.

Tonya Plant sipped her wine alone. The investigators had finished with her room, but she didn't seem in a hurry to return to it. She looked more contented than grief-stricken.

I watched her and wondered about their relationship. They seemed a happy couple, but no one really knew what went on in a marriage besides the two people in it. That was especially the case for public figures like the Plants.

I doubted that Tonya had the physical strength to harm him. He could have easily disarmed her. The same held true for Aunt Pearl, though my aunt was a witch and could summon supernatural strength at the tap of a wand. She had no reason to, though.

Only a man similar in height to Sebastien Plant could have done it, since some of Plant's wounds were on top of his head.

I knew from watching crime shows that eighty percent of victims were murdered by their spouse. Tonya could have gotten someone to kill her husband. If she knew of Sebastien and Hazel's affair, she had a strong motive. As Sebastien's wife she had to be a suspect, but I wasn't sure if the sheriff knew of the affair or not.

One thing I was certain of was that Tonya was no grieving widow, and I intended to prove it.

# CHAPTER 15

*J*t was almost ten p.m. when I arrived at Pearl's Charm
School. My spirits lifted when I saw the lights on. Aunt
Pearl was safely inside and out of trouble, at least for the moment.
As I grew closer I spotted a neon sign in the shape of a broom in the
front window. Beneath the green broom flashed *Open-Open-Open* in
neon white.

Aunt Pearl's hatred for highway signs didn't seem to extend to
her own shingle. She was anything but subtle. I didn't like Aunt
Pearl's obvious flaunting of a school for witches, but it was nice to
see the old schoolhouse put to good use.

As I pushed the door open a bell jingled to announce my arrival.
The old schoolhouse looked much the same as I remembered from
my elementary school days. Even the paint and linoleum were
unchanged.

"In here." My aunt's voice echoed down the hallway and I
followed it into the first classroom. The school was built in the early
1900s with two classrooms, plenty for the population in those days.
It had closed a few years back once we could no longer afford our

own school staff. Nowadays local children were bused to the big school at Shady Creek, a sad sign of the times.

Aunt Pearl was busy lighting votive candles on the windowsill.

"What is it with you and fire?" I walked towards the front of the class and took in my surroundings. I had to admit that the candle-light gave the room a certain ambiance. It was, in a word, charming.

I wasn't about to admit that to Aunt Pearl though.

"Oh, Cen, relax. Do you have to be so serious all the time?"

"Maybe I wouldn't be if I didn't have to constantly bail you out of trouble." Honestly, Aunt Pearl amounted to a full-time job some-times. And I had enough problems of my own right now.

"I'm not in any trouble, and I can take care of myself. Stop worrying about me," Aunt Pearl said.

"You're in plenty of trouble. If I don't worry about you, you'll destroy our little business before it even gets off the ground," I said. "Why did you lie and say you were with Mom? She said you weren't. You don't have an alibi, do you?"

Aunt Pearl rolled her eyes and let out an exaggerated sigh. "You just never let up, Cen."

"This is important, Aunt Pearl. If we don't steer the investigation in another direction you could be charged with murder."

"Fine." She crossed her arms and glared at me. "I was with Hazel. She arrived this morning."

"I don't believe you. You two aren't even speaking to each other." I sighed as I thought of my brother. Poor Alan.

"We called a truce, Cen. Tough times called for tough measures."

"What tough times?" I was confused, but I also felt a surge of hope. "Is Hazel still here? Maybe she can change Alan back to his human form."

Aunt Pearl shook her head. "No, things were never fine. There's something very serious going on, and Travel Unraveled is right at the center of it. We had to stop the development."

"About Alan, I know he's anxious—"

"Not now, Cen." She raised her hand, palm out in traffic cop fashion. "We're at war."

"We have to run a business here, Aunt Pearl. Sebastien Plant could have brought us huge publicity," I said. "Now we'll be known as the place he was murdered. When did Hazel get here?" Two motivated witches were exponentially worse than a single one.

My aunt shrugged. "I think around nine a.m."

"Right around the time of the murder." I scanned the room but saw no sign of Hazel. "Where is she?"

"She left for London an hour ago."

My shoulders sagged in defeat. Almost back to square one for the investigation and my hope of Alan returning to his human form vanished.

As Sebastien's lover, Hazel also had a powerful motive. Aunt Pearl's alibi didn't count for much, considering it came from another potential suspect. "Did anyone else see you two together?"

"No." Aunt Pearl shook her head. "We basically stayed here and drank coffee, just patching things up."

"That's the most ridiculous lie I've ever heard." I crossed my arms and raised my brows. "You two never sit around. Hazel wouldn't travel halfway around the world just to talk."

"Okay, so maybe we visited the gazebo. Hazel and I followed Sebastien Plant to the gazebo, intending to shame and scare him a little so he would leave town. That's when we saw his attacker, the guy in the black hoodie. We had nothing to do with his murder, I swear. Hazel was so upset by it all that she immediately left town. Tell the sheriff that."

"Why can't you tell him? On second thought, don't. Mentioning Hazel just invites a whole bunch of questions that will expose us as witches. Explaining that she can basically teleport herself here in minutes just complicates things." So did her affair with Sebastien Plant, but I was banking on her innocence too. It seemed easier to find the real killer than prove Hazel and Pearl's innocence. "Tell me what you know about the guy in the black hoodie. He's our only real lead so far."

"It's been a long day, Cen. Let's both get some shut eye." Aunt Pearl stood and ushered me towards the hallway. "I'll hatch a plan to dig ourselves out of this mess."

I raised my arms in protest. Aunt Pearl's plans would almost certainly invite more disaster. On the other hand, any more objections from me only made her uncooperative. "Okay, fine. But I want to talk to Hazel and corroborate your story."

I took one last look around and realized that my aunt been working on the old schoolhouse at about the same time we updated the Inn. She caused a lot of trouble, but she also got things done like nobody's business. Pearl's Charm School looked and felt like a real school. The student desks had all been refinished and there were new school supplies in the shelves that lined the walls. The only difference was the crystal ball on the teacher's desk and a blackboard filled with magic spells instead of arithmetic.

"Is that what I think it is?" I walked over to the blackboard and studied the familiar object in the chalk tray. "I didn't know you had a second wand."

"I don't."

"But your wand was taken for evidence. It's locked up at the police station." My mouth dropped open. "Tell me you didn't remove it."

"Okay, I won't tell you. Time to call it a night." She smiled brightly and steered me towards the door.

"What if your wand held the killer's fingerprints? You might have destroyed the only evidence to clear you from the suspect list." I just hoped that the police had dusted it for prints before Aunt Pearl took it.

She threw her head back and laughed. "It's not evidence, since I had nothing to do with that man's murder. Everyone is focused on the murder, but there's been another serious crime committed. No one gave a hoot about my stolen wand, so I took matters into my own hands and got it back."

"You mean you stole it. That's what you did when you removed it from the police evidence locker." I shook my head. "How can I help you if you won't help yourself?" Evidence tampering had far-reaching consequences.

Aunt Pearl ignored me. "I have a right to my own property."

"It's a bit late for that, but I'm not here to criticize you." I paced back and forth in front of the chalkboard. "There is one thing I need to ask. Did you know about Sebastien Plant's affair with Hazel?"

Aunt Pearl's mouth dropped open in feigned shock. "Really?"

"Don't play games with me. You're covering for Hazel, but Aunt Amber told me everything." I was exaggerating, but if Amber knew about the affair, Hazel's best friend Pearl must have known even more. "That's why the two of you went to the gazebo, isn't it?"

Aunt Pearl pursed her lips and didn't answer right away. "Okay, so I knew about the affair. I don't agree with Hazel's morals, but she would never kill Seb, so I saw no point in mentioning it. I didn't want to complicate things."

"Hazel's lover is murdered on our property and you don't think it worth mentioning?" I repeated the sparse details from Aunt Amber. "What else do you know about Sebastien Plant that you're not telling?"

"He planned to divorce Tonya and marry Hazel." She fondled the filigree star on her wand. "Hazel was worried for Seb's safety, so she asked me to help her keep an eye on him."

"A lot of good that did. I don't believe your story." The two of them were just as unlikely of a couple as Tonya and Sebastien were. Hazel was in her seventies, and Sebastien Plant was about fifty, with a young and attractive thirty-something wife. "Hazel must be forty years older than Tonya."

"Don't be so naive, Cen. Hazel transforms herself just like me and my Carolyn Conroe act. Tonya does it too." She snorted. "Men are so gullible."

My mouth dropped open. "Tonya's a witch?" I flashed back to Mom's comment about Aunt Pearl's wand being attractive to another witch. Had Tonya taken it to prevent retaliation from Aunt Pearl?

Aunt Pearl nodded.

"That's impossible. A witch would have caught on to your Carolyn Conroe sideshow."

"Oh, Tonya knew exactly what I was up to. She just played along for appearances sake. It's hard enough for her to put on the grieving widow act." Aunt Pearl smirked. "She's a mediocre witch, and her magic isn't anything to write home about. She's good at one thing though."

"What's that?"

"Bewitching men." Aunt Pearl tapped her wand on the blackboard. "You could be good at that too, if you put a little effort into it."

"You mean like what you do with your sassy Carolyn Conroe act?"

Aunt Pearl rolled her eyes. "If you spent more time at WICCA and in the magic world then I wouldn't have to explain every little detail to you. But you're finally getting it. Not only is she a witch, but she's also after something we have."

"Are you going to tell me what that is, or do I have to guess that too?"

"Tonya wants the town, Cen. That's the real reason I burned down the highway sign. I couldn't let her find it." She wiped an imaginary tear from her cheek. "I failed miserably."

"Why on earth does she want Westwick Corners? The Plants are billionaires. They practically own the travel industry with their travel shows, books, and resorts. There are tons of better places for a resort than our almost-ghost town." As the words left my mouth it suddenly dawned on me that even I didn't believe in our town's future.

Sad.

Aunt Pearl sighed. "I hope this doesn't take all night. Westwick Corners sits atop one of the earth's energy vortexes. Our vortex isn't nearly as famous as some of the others, like Stonehenge and Sedona, Arizona. We like to keep it secret. In fact, that's why the West family originally settled here. It magnifies our powers. You follow so far?"

I nodded. I vaguely knew of the energy vortex, but the lore about special powers and portals to other dimensions or worlds bordered on ridiculous to me. "I don't see how destroying a highway sign would deter her. Any decent witch would be drawn to an energy vortex."

"Only if she's close enough to feel the energy. That's why I'm against tourism, Cen. I tried my hardest to keep her far away, but it wasn't enough. Now it's too late." Aunt Pearl's tears were real this time. "Tonya's Travel Unraveled mega resort will turn Westwick Corners into the Las Vegas of the spirit world, just another vacation stop on the supernatural superhighway.

"Everything that exists today will be torn down and paved over. I love this place, Cen. I'd rather die than watch our little piece of paradise ruined."

I had never seen Aunt Pearl so emotional before, but she was obviously off her rocker. "If anything, Travel Unraveled would have revitalized our entire town. They'll attract more people even if they promote the vortex. We'll all be better off."

"A resort for witches, Cen. The whole supernatural world will descend upon us. Our town is too fragile to be overrun by supernatural beings. It'll be a nightmare. You have no idea how bad that will be."

"But the other Travel Unraveled destination resorts aren't for witches."

Aunt Pearl just stared at me and shook her head. "You've got so much to learn, Cen. I just hope it's not too late."

# CHAPTER 16

*I* kept my promise to Mom and escorted Aunt Pearl back to the Inn before heading home. I had no way of ensuring that Aunt Pearl remained at the Inn, but it was the best I could do. After everything she had told me, I expected more trouble, especially with Aunt Pearl and Tonya under the same roof. Something terrible was bound to happen.

I trudged through the garden towards home. I had always loved the seclusion of my tree house at the rear of the property, but tonight the isolation made me uneasy. After all, a murderer was on the loose.

I was glad that Hazel and Pearl had patched things up, but also feared that the two of them might have unleashed something that couldn't be undone. I planned to call Hazel first thing in the morning and get an account of her visit and the strange man at the gazebo. She would either corroborate Aunt Pearl's version, or I would catch both of them in a lie. The attacker in the black hoodie running across the lawn could be just a fabrication, but I had nothing else to go on.

By the time I reached my place I was half asleep on my feet. It had been a long day. I trudged up the wooden spiral staircase that led home. My tree house nestled in a massive oak tree. Over the years the original structure had been modified and added to as the branches it nestled within allowed. The tree had grown too; one of the branches actually grew into the living room.

I considered Aunt Pearl's comments about Sebastien Plant wanting a divorce. That gave Tonya a pretty solid motive for murder. But if she had committed the crime, she certainly couldn't have done it alone. Sebastien was twice her size, for one thing.

I flashed back to the note left at the crime scene. I could see the block printing as clearly in my mind as if the note was right in front of me. I mouthed the first few lines as I reached the top of the staircase:

THOUGH YOU TRAVEL FAR *and wide,*
*You'd be best to run and hide,*
*Your business was built on travel,*
*But it is here that you become unravelled*

I FROZE on the porch landing as I pondered the British spelling.

Hazel was British.

Aunt Pearl was not.

Hazel's visit coincided with the murder. While she seemed incapable of murder, I didn't really know her that well. Maybe she had done it after all.

I shivered and pushed open the heavy wooden door. As I stepped across the threshold, I decided to forget about everything and call it a night. I was dead on my feet and it was already late. For the next few hours at least, I could escape into my rustic fairy tale castle and forget about the world. All I wanted was my cozy bed and some shut-eye. All my problems would still be waiting for me tomorrow.

I saw a flash of black and white as Alan ran to the door, wagging his little Border collie tail. At least someone was happy to see me. I felt a pang of guilt as he herded me into the kitchen and tapped his dish with his paw.

I had left extra food for him when I left early this morning, but I had never expected to be gone this long. Poor Alan. I refilled his dish and water bowl and watched him wolf down his dinner as I thought about Hazel. I had last seen her a month ago, when she and Pearl had their disagreement.

Alan gave me the perfect excuse to contact Hazel. I could plead to have Alan changed back into his human form, and along the way, find out more about her whereabouts at the time of the murder.

"Thank goodness you're finally home!" A ghostly apparition floated in the kitchen doorway.

My heart stopped cold until I remembered that Grandma Vi, a.k.a. Violet West, had moved in with me yesterday afternoon under heavy protest. Her former suite at the Inn was now a guest room. We were temporary roommates until I moved out of the tree house and in with Brayden in a few weeks' time. Neither of us liked the arrangement, but there were simply no other options.

"You waited up for me?" I felt a tug of tenderness at the thought.

"Don't be silly, Cen. Ghosts don't sleep." Grandma Vi sniffed. "Where are your towels? I can't find a damn thing in this mess. You're so unorganized."

"You're a ghost. Why do you need a towel?" Grandma Vi had passed two years ago and promptly returned to haunt us. In all that time she had never asked for a towel. I suspected she just wanted an excuse to snoop through my things without being obvious. Not that ghosts were the least bit obvious, of course.

Grandma Vi sighed and shook her head. "You wouldn't understand. Your cluttered mind is just like this cluttered house. Nothing is where it belongs."

"Towels are in the linen closet."

"I am not going in there." Grandma Vi hovered in front of me and blocked my path.

Why a ghost who traveled through walls was afraid of a closet was beyond me. "Suit yourself. Anything else?" All I wanted was a few minutes of peace and quiet to unwind before bed.

Grandma Vi threw her ghostly arms in the air. "That closet's a mess. Maybe you did pick the right profession after all."

"What's that supposed to mean?" After a frustrating day with the wedding rehearsal, Pearl's antics at the Inn's grand opening, and of course, Plant's murder, I just wanted to fall into bed and go to sleep. I turned sideways to slip past Grandma Vi.

Grandma Vi refused to let me by, though technically I could walk right through her transparent form. But I respected my elders, even if they didn't respect me.

"You have so many questions but never any answers. Aren't journalists supposed to have both?" She lowered her hands and stepped aside to let me pass. "Ooh...you're thinking about a man, and it's not Brayden."

Grandma Vi is—or at least was—a witch like the rest of us, but since becoming a ghost she could also read minds. In my tired state I had let down my guard and forgotten to block my thoughts. I hadn't even realized I was thinking about him.

It was hard not to imagine Tyler Gates' tightly muscled body underneath his sheriff's uniform. "Just the new sheriff. He started today," I said in my most innocent-sounding voice. I wasn't sure if Grandma Vi saw the images in my head or just the words, but it was creepy knowing she could read my innermost thoughts.

"We have a murder on our hands." I recounted the gazebo encounter, including Pearl's magic wand. I omitted Aunt Pearl's comments on Tonya and the resort plans because I didn't want to upset her.

Grandma Vi hovered behind me as I removed my shoes and headed down the hall to the living room. "I'd better go do some reconnaissance." She sounded eager for something to do.

"No, Grandma. Leave it to the police." I switched topics. "Mom's worried about the impact on our hotel business."

Grandma Vi smiled. "Maybe I'll get my old room back after all."

"I doubt it." The murder would kill our business before it even started. Now we'd never recoup the renovation expenses. The only way Grandma Vi could have remained at the Inn was to room with Aunt Pearl. Their bickering would only invite unwanted attention and Grandma Vi was bound to wander around and scare the guests.

I changed the subject. "The Inn looks absolutely gorgeous." We had taken pains to make the restoration as authentic as possible, right down to the stained-glass windows and restored fir floors. "It looks just like new."

"I wouldn't know." She sniffed. "I'm banished, help captive in this stupid tree. It's persecution if you ask me."

"It's all for the best, Grandma. We need to somehow earn a living, and this is all we've got. You're free to visit anytime once the guests leave. It looks just like the old days when you lived there."

"Exactly how old you think I am? The place was old when I lived there too." Even in death, Grandma Vi was sensitive about her age.

"You're not old at all. Just older than me." I headed into the living room to the sofa.

"Enough age-bashing. Let's get back to the murder. It's too dangerous to hold your wedding here, Cen. You should cancel it." Grandma and Brayden didn't get along. But Grandma Vi was dead to Brayden since he couldn't see ghosts. So in fact it was only Grandma Vi that didn't get along.

"I am not canceling my wedding. Why would I do that?" At least Grandma hadn't read my mind about that yet. I flopped down on the sofa, exhausted.

She shrugged. "One can hope." Her form gradually solidified as she floated across the room and hovered over me.

I recounted the rest of today's events, including Pearl's highway pyrotechnic demonstration and her Carolyn Conroe antics. "She needs to tone things down before she drives away another sheriff. We can't have a lawless town. Can you talk to her?"

"I'll see what I can do. Now tell me about this new sheriff."

97

I described the showdown in my office and Aunt Pearl's grudging acceptance of her fine. "He seemed to hold his own against Pearl, though. She can't just light things on fire whenever things don't go her way." Tyler Gates was the first sheriff that had really stood up to Aunt Pearl. Maybe he would last after all.

Grandma Vi sighed. "Tell her to come see me."

# CHAPTER 17

*J* had just drifted off to sleep when I awoke to barking outside my window.

"Wake up, Cen." Grandma Vi hovered above me. She waved her transparent arms back and forth. "Open the window. Alan's outside."

I complied and looked down to see Alan running in circles and yelping. I didn't remember letting him outside.

Alan growled and ran a few feet towards the vineyard, reversed course and ran back under the window. He looked up at us with pleading eyes.

"I can't see in the dark. Just a sec." I scrambled out of bed and grabbed a flashlight from my nightstand before heading to the front door. Grandma Vi floated a few feet behind me. Alan bolted inside as soon as I opened the door. "I sure wish you could talk."

Alan shook his furry canine body and whined as he stared at me.

"What is it?" My voice broke as I thought of how I had just missed Hazel, and the chance to get Alan back to normal, by mere hours. I felt bad for my brother.

Alan paced back and forth before heading into the living room.

"He says go to the window." Apparently Grandma Vi could read canine minds too, or at least a human mind trapped in a canine body.

I followed him into the living room as Grandma Vi floated behind us. I headed to the window and pulled back the curtains. The window provided a direct view of the vineyard. Clouds partially obscured the moon, giving the night sky a hazy glow. It was light enough to illuminate the vineyard in silhouette, but not much else." I don't see anything."

Alan jumped up on the couch and nudged my arm with his nose.

"Over there?" I turned to the right where two shadowy figures stood at the edge of the vineyard, several feet apart. It was too dark to make out any features, other than they were both men with a slim build.

"That's Brayden!" Grandma Vi shook her head. "What on earth is he doing in our vineyard? I never trusted that young man. He's up to no good."

"You can't possibly recognize him from here." I squinted but it made no difference.

"You need to get your eyes checked, Cen. Or maybe you just don't want to face the facts about your beau."

"What facts?" Brayden had never uttered an unkind word to Grandma Vi. I had no idea why she despised him so much.

Grandma Vi ignored me.

"What's Brayden doing with that other guy?" Grandma Vi floated beside us at the window.

"I can't really see—" I strained my eyes but still saw only their profiles in the darkness.

"They're pacing out steps, like a Mexican standoff."

Brayden in a vineyard duel in the dead of night was ridiculous, but now that my eyes had adjusted to the darkness I saw that Grandma was right. I recognized his slow, purposeful gait. He walked in a straight line, carefully counting his steps.

"They're measuring out steps in a big square, Cen. That's exactly the sort of thing people do when they develop a property."

"They do?" It seemed an unreliable method to survey property in this day and age. "As long as it's not twenty paces and a duel, I'm fine with it." I flashed back to the Centralex development plans in Tonya's room and got an uneasy feeling. I still wasn't about to confide in Grandma Vi. I turned away from the window and headed back to my bedroom where my soft bed awaited me.

"Hold on, Cen. I hope you're not adding even more businesses around here without telling me." She sniffled. "It's bad enough getting kicked out of my own house and exiled to this messy tree fort. I guess even this tree will be cut down to make way for the asphalt jungle. I'll be homeless." Her apparition wavered the way it did when she was really upset.

"Nothing of the sort is happening," I said. "They must have stepped outside for some fresh air." But Brayden's after midnight walk aroused my suspicions too. He avoided exercise whenever possible, including leisurely walks. Everything had a purpose with him. Grandma Vi was right. Something fishy was going on.

"Here comes the other guy." Grandma Vi pointed to a man about fifty feet away from Brayden. He reversed course and started walking back towards Brayden. Once he reached Brayden it was clear that he was a few inches taller, with longer, shoulder-length hair. He wasn't a local or anyone I recognized.

"They're definitely measuring something. I don't like it either," I said. There was no reason at all for Brayden to be showing our property to a stranger.

Alan growled in agreement, then laid down on the floor.

Grandma looked sympathetically at him. "Poor thing, you must be exhausted."

I padded to the kitchen and rummaged through my fridge. I found a bone for Alan to chew on. "I'll ask Brayden about it tomorrow." Just before I break his heart. The thought brought back my bad mood. Suddenly I wasn't sleepy anymore.

"One more thing, Cen."

"Now what?"

"I know what your secret is." Grandma taunted me like a third grader on Valentine's Day. "You were dreaming about him."

"You're trespassing into my dreams?" My new roommate was overstepping her boundaries, and I didn't like it one bit. It was tolerable for a couple of weeks, but if I called off the wedding, this could be permanent. We had to figure out some different living arrangements.

"You have a crush, and it's not Brayden." She tittered like a schoolgirl.

"I don't know what you're talking about." I closed my eyes and tried to ignore her.

"That new sheriff sure is a looker. Why not hook up with him instead?" She gave me a ghostly smile.

I felt my face flush. I wasn't hooking up with anyone, let alone Tyler Gates. My physical attraction to him was natural for any red-blooded American woman, wasn't it? I told myself that's all it was, but I couldn't get him out of my mind. As sleep overtook me, my thoughts drifted to my wedding. Only this time, the groom wasn't Brayden Banks.

# CHAPTER 18

*I* awoke just before seven, exhausted after a mostly sleepless night. I opened a can of Alan's favorite dog food and scooped out a double helping to make up for getting home late yesterday. I vowed to somehow convince Hazel to return and make things right for my brother.

My stomach growled as I inhaled the stinky dog food. I craved caffeine, eggs, and toast. As a ghost, Grandma Vi didn't eat, so I decided to head over to the Inn for breakfast. A hearty meal was exactly what I needed to get my investigative juices flowing.

I glanced over at Alan who had already devoured his food and waited impatiently by the door. I let him out as I recalled last night's events.

Brayden's secret visit troubled me, and it reminded me of Aunt Pearl's comments about Tonya. I didn't think Brayden and Tonya knew each other, but their shared interest in our property seemed too coincidental. I intended to get to the bottom of it.

I left Grandma Vi and Alan on lookout duty and promised to check back in a few hours. Neither Grandma nor Alan could pick up a phone, so that meant doubling back to the tree house later in the morning. I convinced Grandma Vi that Alan needed company. It was the only way to persuade her to stay at the tree house. With everything going on, Grandma Vi was itching to visit the Inn, but that would just complicate matters.

I passed the vineyard and crossed the garden on my walk to the Inn. My heart did a somersault when I spotted Tyler Gates' SUV parked in the lot. I smoothed my hair, regretting my wardrobe choice of a baggy t-shirt, shorts, sneakers and no make-up. I got a weird fluttery feeling in my stomach, something I couldn't remember experiencing before.

I slowed my walk and reviewed my goals for today. I had a lot on my to-do list. First on the list was to investigate Tonya and validate Aunt Pearl's claims about the vortex and confirm that she was a witch. The development plans proved she was eying our property, but that didn't make her a killer.

A close second was talking to Hazel. Her visit coincided exactly with Sebastien and Tonya's, all the more suspicious considering their love triangle. Was Hazel acting in her official WICCA capacity as Aunt Pearl claimed, or had she come to Westwick Corners for personal reasons? I was betting on the latter. I was also angry with Hazel. If she had reconciled with Aunt Pearl, the least she could have done was immediately reverse Alan's curse.

In short, I would conduct my own probe in parallel with the police investigation. Only I would focus on the supernatural elements while the sheriff tackled the regular ones. The sheriff didn't know this of course.

Key to both our investigations was finding the man in the black hoodie. I had nothing to go on, but I had to start somewhere. Maybe I'd press the sheriff for more information on the mysterious man as a pretext for a story. I just hoped he was following up on that lead.

Meanwhile Aunt Pearl continued to incriminate herself. On top of everything else, I needed to get the heat off of suspect number one, Aunt Pearl. As long as her alibi with Hazel checked out, I was pretty confident I could steer the investigation back in the right direction. Hazel was less evasive than my aunt, so as long as she cooperated, I could probably clear them both.

If they were innocent, of course.

Aunt Pearl's nuggets of intelligence led me to believe she wasn't involved, but the only way to steer the official investigation onto the real killer was to find a lead, whether that was Tonya, the guy in the black hoodie, or someone else. A good lead got my aunt off the hook and also ensured justice was served on the real killer.

Last but not least, I had to do whatever I could to ensure Tyler Gates stayed on the job. I didn't want the sheriff to quit our town, but the supernatural elements could prove to be too much for him.

Aunt Pearl's revelation about Tonya gave the case a whole new angle. The sorcery world was small, yet somehow I had never met, or even heard of Tonya. I needed to dig into her past.

I was so lost in thought that I collided with Aunt Pearl as I crossed the driveway.

"Hey!" Aunt Pearl balanced on one leg before regaining her balance. "Watch where you're going."

"Sorry." I glanced towards the Inn's dining room windows, hoping that no one, especially not Sheriff Gates, had noticed Aunt Pearl's agile balancing act and recovery. It would be doubly hard to explain the wand away as a cane if he had witnessed our collision and my aunt's advanced yoga moves.

"Time for class." Aunt Pearl motioned for me to follow her.

"Can't it wait till after breakfast?" I regretted my late night promise but there wasn't much I could do about it now. I was trapped. She had obviously been lying in wait for me, since she wasn't an early riser.

Aunt Pearl shook her head. "It has to be now. I've got some more intel on Tonya."

My heart raced as I imagined the worst. "Don't tell me you went back to her room."

"Not exactly, no."

"Can you be more specific?"

Aunt Pearl looked around to make sure no one was within earshot. "Not here. Follow me."

# CHAPTER 19

*a*n hour later I squirmed in my seat in the first row of the classroom at Pearl's Charm School. I struggled to both stay conscious and hold my temper. I was sleep deprived, ravenously hungry and my involuntary caffeine withdrawal was giving me a headache.

I was no closer to finding out Aunt Pearl's revelations about Tonya. She refused to divulge any details until I completed my first magic lesson. Another one of her tricks.

Aunt Pearl tapped her wand on the blackboard. "And that's how you do a reversal spell. Got it?"

I nodded, though I was so distracted with my growing to-do list that I had missed a few steps.

"Let's see you do it."

I frowned. "Can we do this later? We should focus on solving Plant's murder instead."

"Uh-uh, missy. Now or never." She tapped the tip of her wand on her palm.

"You need to return that wand, Aunt Pearl. It's evidence."

"It's nothing of the sort. It's my spare wand."

"But last night you said you had taken it from the evidence locker."

"I said nothing of the sort. You thought that and I didn't bother to correct you. Every good witch has a spare, Cendrine. Always have a backup plan."

"You're just making that up so I stop bugging you about it. You have to give it back to the sheriff, Aunt Pearl."

"I don't know what you're talking about." Aunt Pearl batted her eyelashes. "This wand has been here the whole time."

"I know you don't have two wands. What I don't understand is why you'd want to make up stuff."

Aunt Pearl shook her head slowly. "At first I thought it was my wand in the gazebo. But it wasn't my wand, just a perfect replica. My wand has been here the whole time."

"I don't believe you."

"Think about it, Cen. Of course I had my wand. How else could I have shape-shifted into Carolyn Conroe last night?"

"The bigger question is, why you had to shape shift in the first place."

"Ah-hah! I thought you'd never ask. I had to distract Tonya while Hazel did her thing."

I didn't like where this was going. "What exactly was Hazel doing?"

"Saving Westwick Corners from destruction and ruin."

"You're being overly dramatic." I stood to leave.

Aunt Pearl motioned me to sit back down. "Tonya made a potion to bewitch me, Ruby, Amber, and you. She plans to use it at breakfast. That's why I had to intercept you."

"But what about Mom? She's at the inn cooking breakfast all alone right now. Shouldn't we warn her?"

"Relax. She knows all about it."

It still didn't make sense to me. "Why does she want to use it on me? I'm not an owner." I could see Mom and my aunts being targets, but I didn't have an interest in the property.

"No, but Tonya knows you're a witch. You have influence. She needs to neutralize you, so you can't undo her spell. That's the other reason you're here. You need to brush up on your magic skills if you're going to defend us."

A lump formed in my throat. "Defend you from what?"

"Tonya's potion will take away our free will. We will be completely under her command, unable to think or make decisions for ourselves. She will force us to sign over our property for a pittance. In return we'll be penniless and homeless."

"She can't do that in this day and age, Aunt Pearl. There has to be a bill of sale and title transfer. It won't work."

Aunt Pearl rolled her eyes. "You're getting distracted with all that bureaucratic crap. She'll make it look normal, but that won't be what's really happening. But that's not the worst of it. Once we lose our free will and ability to make choices, she'll force us to make the ultimate choice—to give up our powers."

"I don't see how that's possible. We're born with those powers."

"We are, but because we have free will, we can always choose to forfeit our powers." Her eyes bored into mine. "Sort of like what you're been doing by hiding your talents. You got to use it or lose it, Cen. Tonya's got it all figured out. Except she still doesn't know what we found in her room Friday morning."

"You mean the plans?" I flashed back to our visit to the Plants' room and realized that Aunt Pearl knew a little too much about its contents. "You were in that room a few times before you brought me, weren't you?"

"Nope." Aunt Pearl smiled smugly.

"I just don't understand you sometimes. You said you didn't want Tonya here, but it's almost like you enticed her here. You know a lot more than you're letting on, and I just wish you'd come clean. If you won't tell the sheriff, at least tell me so I can help."

"I had to switch to Plan B," Aunt Pearl said. "You know what Confucius says: keep your friends close and your enemies closer. I checked the Plants in early so I could keep an eye on Tonya."

"I doubt Confucius meant you should invite disaster, but whatever." The only good thing was that if Aunt Pearl really had Tonya under surveillance, she could at least verify some of Tonya's claims.

Aunt Pearl pulled a wrinkled receipt from her pocket and handed it to me. "Look at this. It was lying on the dresser in the Plant's room."

The receipt from the Shady Creek Walmart was dated Thursday at 11:15 p.m. The items on the bill included latex gloves and plastic garbage bags, all purchased in cash.

"You took this from Tonya's room?"

Aunt Pearl nodded. "Actually, Hazel took it. Now we just have to give it to the sheriff without appearing to cooperate."

"We?" If it truly was evidence, Aunt Pearl had compromised it by removing it from Tonya's room. "This is a murder, Aunt Pearl. It's much bigger than your spat with the sheriff. Just give it to him yourself." The sheriff now knew of Tonya and Sebastien Plant's early check-in time, but whether he considered Tonya a prime suspect was quite another matter. I actually felt bad for him, since my aunt was purposely hiding evidence.

"No. I want you to give it to him." She placed the receipt on my desk.

"Why me?"

"I can't stand the sight of that man."

I was losing patience, but someone had to give him a key piece of evidence, and soon. The items certainly looked sinister when purchased together. "Fine. I'll do it."

If Aunt Pearl was right about Tonya, we had no time to waste.

# CHAPTER 20

In true supernatural fashion, Aunt Pearl seemed the most normal when the opposite was true. Witches often exaggerated the ordinary and played down huge events. This was one of those moments, and I feared disaster.

"You've destroyed the chain of custody by taking the evidence, Aunt Pearl. It's no good now."

"That's where you're wrong, Cen. It might not be good in a mortal court of law, but we've got all the evidence we need for a supernatural one. That's the one that counts."

I begged to differ. The Washington courts were very real, and Aunt Pearl's ties stretched easily beyond a doubt. "Uh—because you had already stolen it by then."

"That wand is mine, Cendrine. How can I steal something that was mine to begin with?"

We were talking in circles. Aunt Pearl was hoping to confuse me so I'd change the subject. It wasn't working.

"Ah-hah! You did steal it after all." I shook my head in exasperation. "How can I help you if you won't cooperate?"

Aunt Pearl said nothing as she studied her feet.

"Just tell me the truth, Aunt Pearl. I promise I won't report you to WICCA." Aunt Pearl always skated on the thin edge of WICCA regulations. It was a constant source of embarrassment for Aunt Amber, who felt her younger sister's constant rule-bending and breaking tarnished the West family reputation.

"Report me for what? I haven't done anything." Aunt Pearl batted her eyelashes and gave me her most innocent look.

"There's something you're not telling me. I can tell by your expression."

"That's ridiculous."

I pulled out my cell phone. "Lost wands are serious, especially when they fall into the hands of non-witches. I'm calling Aunt Amber and telling her what happened. She'll know what to do."

"Cen, stop." Aunt Pearl paced in front of the blackboard. "Please don't call Amber. Just don't. She'll throw the book at me."

I put my phone back in my purse. "Start talking. Tell me how your wand ended up at the murder scene."

"I have no idea. That wand must be a duplicate—a fake. You've got to believe me, Cen. It's not my wand."

That was easy to prove. "I'll just call Sheriff Gates and confirm that. If you're telling the truth, he should still have the fake wand in the police evidence locker." I had no intention of calling him but Aunt Pearl didn't know that.

"No—wait. I was at the gazebo, waiting for you and Ruby. I saw the whole thing."

"I thought you and Mom walked over together."

"That was later. I returned to the Inn after the fight," Aunt Pearl explained. "I went to the gazebo a few minutes early, hoping to practice a few minutes of magic before everyone else arrived. I saw it happen."

"You saw the murder?"

"Yes," she whispered. Her face turned a ghostly white. "I just thought it was a fight. I didn't know he died."

"Once you knew it was murder, you still didn't tell the sheriff.

Why?" It suddenly dawned on me that she had kept it secret from one other person. "You didn't tell Mom, either, did you? You walked all the way back to the Inn, brought her back with you knowing that someone was injured or dying in the gazebo."

"No, Cen." Aunt Pearl frowned as she rubbed her forehead. "I didn't know anyone was dead. I saw two men fighting, so I hid in the laurel hedge. When the shouting stopped, I saw one man walk away. I assumed the other one had already left. I had no idea he was there, much less dead. Had I known, I would have tried to help."

This time I believed her. "What did this man look like?"

"I can't remember. It just happened so fast."

"But you were there."

Aunt Pearl nodded. A single tear fell down her cheek.

"Then there's nothing to worry about," I said.

"Huh?"

"We can do a reversal spell and unlock the truth."

"Oh."

She was lying again. "You weren't actually there, were you?"

"Not exactly," Aunt Pearl said. "There was a break-in here at the school yesterday." She pointed to a broken windowpane in the door. "Somebody stole my wand while I was in the bathroom. I chased him to the gazebo, but it was too late."

The image of Aunt Pearl running down a criminal flashed before me. That, and the odds of a daytime break-and-enter in our town were next to zero probability, but then so was the murder. "Why didn't you mention this sooner? What did the intruder look like?" Her fearful expression told me she was telling the truth this time. Leaving a wand unattended was a WICCA no-no. I guessed that my aunt had covered up to avoid WICCA backlash and a fine.

"I couldn't get a good look, Cen. But it was a man, wearing a black hoodie. That part's the truth. I only saw him from behind."

"Tall, short, fat, skinny? You must at least know that."

"I don't know...maybe a few inches shorter than Sebastien Plant."

Sebastien Plant was about six-foot-four, so the other man was probably about six feet in height. "So you followed him to the gazebo. Then what?"

"Sebastien Plant was already there. He argued with the guy in the hoodie. They fought and suddenly Plant went down."

I prayed Aunt Pearl wasn't lying again. "What were they arguing about?"

"I wasn't close enough to make out the words. Like I said earlier, when I heard them fighting, I hid in the hedge."

An image of Aunt Pearl crawling in the shrubbery on all fours flashed through my mind. "Not even a snippet of conversation?"

Aunt Pearl shook her head. "Nothing at all."

Selective hearing. Which was weird, considering our supernatural abilities to amplify and all...

Sebastien Plant was famous enough that everyone in town knew about our guest of honor. Anyone against tourism might have a bone to pick with him. Like Aunt Pearl.

"What happened next?"

"The guy ran away."

"You must have seen his face then, when he turned back towards you."

Aunt Pearl shook her head. "I heard him leave, but I couldn't get a good view from my hiding place in the hedge. I waited a few minutes and then ran back to the Inn. I panicked and even forgot all about getting my wand back. I never set foot in the gazebo, so I didn't know that Plant never got up and left."

My eyes narrowed. Aunt Pearl had most certainly been in the gazebo when I showed up for my pre-rehearsal rehearsal. She must have guessed my conclusion.

"I swear, Cen. I never saw him until you arrived and we both fell on him. I just remembered something though," Aunt Pearl said. "I couldn't make out Plant's words because he was slurring his words and staggering around. It was even worse than when they checked in."

Plant's drunken state increased the possibility of a smaller man knocking him over. That was interesting, but without a description it was next to impossible to narrow down a suspect.

One thing still bothered me though. "You never came back to get your wand?" It was hard to believe she wouldn't have retrieved it right after we tripped over Sebastien Plant's body. She knew it was there and it was too important for it to slip her mind. She was almost certainly still hiding something.

Her wand was of no use to anyone else, at least not for witchcraft. Despite Mom's suspicions, I knew another witch would have difficulty unlocking its powers and wouldn't bother with it. Other than our family, there were no other witches in Westwick Corners. "You never go anywhere without it."

"I was scared. But I still didn't think he was dead, Cen. Maybe knocked out or something. I thought if I said anything, I'd get into more trouble with the sheriff."

"Well you're in a lot of trouble now. You realize that everything points to you?" Aunt Pearl had no alibi, her wand was the murder weapon, and she had a motive: to stop tourism at all costs. But I knew in my heart she wasn't a murderer. "We have to find a way to explain this to the sheriff, without mentioning the magic parts."

"You're going to betray your own flesh and blood?"

"Don't be ridiculous, Aunt Pearl. You have to admit, though, the optics don't look good. Why can't you cooperate?"

"Why should I? If we didn't start this stupid tourism thing, that guy would still be alive."

"Maybe, maybe not. I know one thing for sure, though."

"What?"

"Once we're exposed as witches, life won't be pleasant for any of us."

# CHAPTER 21

"Tell me what you know about Tonya." We had barely finished lesson one when I was duly informed that it was just the first of the seventy-seven Pearls of Witchcraft Wisdom that I had agreed to. I didn't remember agreeing, but fighting with Aunt Pearl wore me out too much to argue. I needed caffeine, and fast. "How come I've never heard of her?"

Aunt Pearl crossed her arm and shook her head. "You've shunned the magic world for so long, Cen. When you don't move in the right circles, you tend to miss a lot of things."

"Okay, fine. I'll pay more attention from now on." I was tired of my aunt's guilt trips, but I was starting to see her point about ignoring my witch heritage. "Tell me what you know about Tonya and Sebastien."

"Tonya's not a very powerful witch. That's probably why you never knew about her supernatural talents. The most dangerous thing about her is her ruthless ambition. Sebastien Plant never had a chance once she set her sights on him. Marrying him was on her to-do list before she even met him."

I knew little about the couple other than they had married after a whirlwind romance. Sebastien Plant had spent decades building Travel Unraveled, and that's where he met Tonya. She worked in the office as a temp before marrying him less than a year later.

Aunt Pearl tapped her wand on the blackboard and everything erased. "Tonya got very involved in Travel Unraveled once they were married. Remember that invitation you sent to Sebastien Plant all those months ago?"

I nodded.

"Sebastien wasn't interested, which is why you never got a reply. Tonya came across the invitation months later. She researched our town and found historical records that mentioned Westwick Corners and the energy vortex. It had been forgotten over the years, but the invitation just resurrected interest. Tonya thought Travel Unraveled should do a major development here. Sebastien vetoed the idea, and soon after they began to have marriage problems."

"How do you know all this?" It would have been useful if she shared the information earlier.

"Hazel told me."

"Hazel was having an affair with him. Of course she's going to say they had marriage problems. She probably exaggerated the other stuff too." I jerked around in my seat, certain I had heard a cough. "Did you hear that?"

Aunt Pearl shook her head. "That's not how Hazel knows about the development. Tonya approached her about relocating WICCA headquarters to Westwick Corners, but Hazel said no."

"I thought Sebastien had already vetoed any development. Did he change his mind?" Tonya probably wanted to pre-sell the development to convince Sebastien. Energy vortexes made for more effective magic, which was both good and bad. One thing was certain: our peaceful existence would be no more.

"No. He had no idea that Tonya was a witch and he knew nothing about WICCA."

It struck me as curious that Sebastien Plant was oblivious to witches, yet had been romantically linked to two of them. I started to see the picture. "Tonya wanted to take over the town first, and then WICCA. She went ahead anyway, knowing Sebastien didn't agree. She could either change his mind, or..."

Aunt Pearl finished my sentence. "Get rid of him. That's why Tonya told Sebastien that she had accidentally accepted our invitation, months after you sent it. At least that's what Seb told Hazel. It was an excuse to check the place out. And a place to kill her husband. What better place than a small town to kill her husband and pin it on someone else?"

I nodded. "She thinks the small town police will bungle the investigation, and no one will care much about a stranger, even a famous one."

Strangely, it all made sense. Except for one thing. "When did you and Hazel stop fighting?" Maybe Hazel had called the truce to establish an alibi or something.

Aunt Pearl shrugged. "What does it matter?"

"It matters a lot. Hazel's involvement in a love triangle with the murder victim gives her a motive. She might not even have an alibi." I recounted Aunt Amber's comment about having last seen Hazel at six p.m. London time, which equated to nine hours earlier, or nine a.m. in local Westwick Corners time. Since travel time for a witch was practically instantaneous, Hazel also had the means to kill Sebastien, and her whereabouts were unaccounted for. Another suspect.

Great.

"Except the killer was a man, not a woman," Aunt Pearl pointed out.

"You're absolutely sure about that? You said you didn't get a good look at the person in the hoodie."

"I saw enough to know it was a man," Aunt Pearl said.

"Too bad Hazel's not here. Maybe she could shed some light on this."

"Ask me anything." Witch Hazel stood in the doorway, looking every one of her seventy years. She wore a track suit almost identical to Aunt Pearl's, except for sequined stripes that ran down the outside seams of her pant legs. A black beret rested jauntily atop her silver hair. I guessed she wasn't in her alter ego right now. "What are you doing here?"

"Trying to save the town, just like Pearl." Hazel tapped her wand on the wooden floorboards as if shaking out the cobwebs. "Speaking of which, we could sure use your help."

# CHAPTER 22

$\mathcal{I}$ still reeled from the shock of seeing Witch Hazel. She and Aunt Pearl stood together at the blackboard looking like fast friends. It was obvious they had patched things up and they were back to normal. Well, at least what constituted normal for them. I was just relieved their months-long feud had ended.

"We've decided to let bygones be bygones." Hazel beamed as she looked at Pearl.

"That's great news," I said. "While you're here, you can change Alan back to his human form. He'll be so excited."

"We'll deal with Alan later. First things first." Aunt Pearl dismissed me with a wave. "We don't have much time to stop Tonya."

But I had questions for Hazel that couldn't wait. "You were here all day Friday?" That changed everything, since Hazel was here at the time of Plant's murder.

It also meant that not one, but three witches had motives to kill Plant.

Hazel nodded. "I was with Pearl since about 9:30 Friday morning."

"She's my alibi, Cen. I couldn't tell the sheriff, because Hazel made me promise not to tell anyone she was in town."

I brightened at the thought of Aunt Pearl's alibi, but just as quickly realized it meant almost nothing. "You both have a motive to kill Sebastien. You want to quash tourism and Hazel is—or was—part of a love triangle. You two could be accomplices rather than each other's alibis."

Hazel shook her head. "Seb planned to leave Tonya for me. She can't find out that I'm here. At least not until we can disable her. She's very dangerous right now."

"I thought you said she wasn't a very good witch? Surely you can overpower her."

"We can, but we can't overcome public opinion. She's very good at manipulating the facts and getting people—and witches—on her side. People don't realize that she uses deadly methods to get results. We have to pin the crime on her, and we need your help, Cen. You need to expose her as the killer."

"Why me? Just talk to the sheriff and come clean." I didn't want to get involved in any of their crazy plans. "Aunt Pearl, you checked them in. If Sebastien was so drunk, what was he doing out walking alone in the middle of the night?"

"Sebastien drunk?" Hazel grabbed Aunt Pearl's arm. "That's impossible. He never touches the stuff."

"He was definitely drunk," Pearl grumbled. "He slurred his words and could barely stand."

"Yet he walked to the gazebo," I said. "He was still drunk hours later when he argued and fought with the mystery man in the gazebo. If he was in such bad shape, how did he even make it to the gazebo in the first place?" Most drunks just passed out.

"Tonya did something to him, I just know it," Hazel said. "You've got to get the sheriff to investigate her."

"I'll do no such thing," I said. "Aunt Pearl, you have to come clean with the sheriff. You're just wasting his time with your avoidance tactics and making yourself look guilty in the process."

My aunt just shook her head and looked expectantly at Hazel. That was the weird thing about their relationship. Aunt Pearl never deferred to anyone, but she respected Hazel immensely.

"We're not asking you to do anything deceitful," Hazel said. "Just steer the sheriff in the right direction, and we'll take care of all the background stuff."

"What do you mean by background stuff?" I worried about what they were up to. But sometimes knowledge was a dangerous thing.

"You don't want to know, Cen. Don't ask, don't tell," said Aunt Pearl.

I reluctantly agreed to put our plan into action just as soon as I had some breakfast. One thing was crystal clear. I had to get to the bottom of things before Sheriff Tyler Gates did.

# CHAPTER 23

*J*followed Aunt Pearl into the Inn's dining room, still grumpy from losing almost two hours from my day right from the start at Pearl's Charm School. It had yielded interesting results, but at the expense of my breakfast. I was ravenously hungry, and ready to commit criminal acts for a dose of caffeine.

Except I couldn't risk eating in the dining room if Aunt Pearl's and Hazel's claims about Tonya's potion were true. My stomach rumbled in protest.

I reached in my pocket and fingered the Walmart receipt. I reviewed the items in my mind and stopped short at the antifreeze. Antifreeze's main ingredient was ethylene glycol, a toxic substance that also happened to be alcohol. It was a lethal form of alcohol, but it probably produced the same symptoms as an excess of booze.

Sebastien Plant didn't drink alcohol, but perhaps he had unknowingly ingested antifreeze. I flashed back to the trash from the Plants room. What if the half-empty bottle of lemon-lime Gatorade wasn't what it seemed?

The Walmart receipt burned a hole in my pocket, and I was anxious to hand it over to the sheriff. I didn't want to follow Aunt

123

Pearl's lead and withhold evidence, especially a potential clue removed from the Plants' room. It was a very good clue, since Walmart stores also had surveillance cameras. Though we had removed the receipt, the cameras could still trace the purchase back to Tonya.

Aunt Pearl headed straight for the kitchen, and I made a beeline for the small counter outside the kitchen door. I inhaled the rich aroma of freshly brewed coffee and poured myself a nice steaming mugful.

At last.

I sipped my strong black coffee and scanned the room. I almost choked when I spied Sheriff Tyler Gates sitting at a window table. I started to walk towards his table to give him the Walmart receipt when I saw that he wasn't alone.

He sat across from Tonya Plant in the dining room, his back to me. Tonya's face was clearly visible. At first glance she appeared grief-stricken. I wouldn't have given her a second look if not for Hazel and Aunt Pearl's accusations.

She dabbed her eyes with a tissue, but even from twenty feet away I noticed her perfectly made-up face and hair. Judging from her body language, she didn't seem hysterical or even look like she had been crying. And she had eaten all of her eggs Benedict. Everyone handled grief differently, but few grieving spouses finished a hearty breakfast.

I tried to imagine how I would feel if something happened to Brayden. Even now, with my second thoughts on the wedding, I couldn't imagine sitting down for breakfast if something had happened to him. I would be inconsolable with grief, unable to speak or function. I definitely wouldn't be scraping hollandaise sauce off my plate.

My stomach growled until I remembered Tonya's secret plans to bewitch us with her magic potion that removed our powers. I couldn't risk eating something that could be tainted. My mouth dropped open as I realized she could have spiked the coffee I had just drank. I grimaced as I thought of Sebastien Plant and the antifreeze.

The coffee station was in the dining room just outside the kitchen door. It was easily accessible by all the guests. Surely she wouldn't slip her potion into the coffee where other guests could drink it too.

Why not? The potion didn't affect anyone other than witches. I felt a bitter taste in my mouth as I realized I had already ingested some of the coffee.

I placed my mug on the counter as I watched them at the table. I strained to hear their conversation, but it was impossible over the din of the dining room.

I grabbed the coffee carafe and headed towards their table. Tonya's breakfast plate was empty as was the breadbasket. She swirled her half-empty coffee cup absent-mindedly as she talked. Sheriff Plant had only an empty coffee cup in front of him.

"Mrs. Plant, I'm very sorry to hear about your husband. Would you like some coffee?"

Tonya nodded.

I picked up Tonya's coffee cup in slow motion, determined to remain at the table as long as possible.

Tonya turned back to the sheriff and let out a small sniffle. "As I was saying, I didn't even realize he was gone. I was busy unpacking. I had insomnia the previous night, so I decided to have a nap. I took a sleeping pill and fell asleep within minutes. He was still in the room when I fell asleep."

"So you were in your room by yourself?" I refilled Tonya's cup.

Tyler Gates glared at me. "I'll ask the questions if you don't mind."

I turned to the sheriff's empty coffee cup and refilled it as slowly as possible, the dark liquid a mere trickle. "Anything else I can get you?"

Tonya Plant sipped her coffee and looked up at me. "Maybe a small plate of fruit I can take to my room."

I exhaled a huge sigh of relief. The coffee wasn't tainted since Tonya had just drank it.

I stared at her empty plate. She had a very healthy appetite considering she had just lost her husband.

Sheriff Gates looked up at me questioningly.

"Yes?" I waited.

"Don't you have other things to do? You must be extremely busy."

I shook my head. "Not really." I needed to hover as long as possible. If Tonya Plant's claim of being asleep was true, it was understandable that she might be short on details. But that also made her short an alibi.

"Thanks, Cendrine." Sheriff Gates spoke a little louder than necessary as he waved me away.

I reluctantly headed into the kitchen, where Mom and Aunt Pearl talked in hushed tones by the grill.

"Did you find anything out, Cen?" Mom was a worrier, but in this case she wasn't overreacting. The Westwick Corners Inn was in jeopardy in more ways than one. Still, I got the distinct impression that my aunt hadn't spilled the beans about Hazel.

"Tonya said she was sleeping and wasn't aware Sebastien had left the room." My stomach grumbled as I inhaled the eggs and bacon breakfast aromas from the grill.

"Sleeping where? They only checked in a few hours ago," Mom said.

I looked at Aunt Pearl's guilty expression and decided to call her on it. "You know more than you're saying again. What time did they check in?"

"Late last night," Pearl said.

"That's impossible," Mom said. "We just officially opened a few hours ago with our very first guests."

Aunt Pearl shrugged. "Today's our official grand opening, and that's when they officially checked in. But they arrived around one in the morning. You were asleep. I heard them at the door and let them in. I gave them a room and just told them to come to the front desk later in the morning."

"That's a pretty big detail to leave out, Pearl. We had our VIP guests here and we didn't even know it. Something terrible could have happened."

"It did," I pointed out.


MOM MASSAGED her forehead like she was getting a migraine. "Why didn't you mention this before? We have a business to run. You can't just fly by the seat of your pants."

At least Aunt Pearl had finally come clean with Mom. I hated secrets and resented being pulled into my aunt's intrigue. True, Mom was a worrier, but we were all in this together, and she deserved to know everything that was going on.

Mom liked process, procedure, and things to run smoothly. Aunt Pearl was her lifelong nervous breakdown in waiting.

I waved my hand in dismissal. "What's done is done. Let's focus on Sebastien Plant's activities. According to Tonya, he was gone when she awoke around eight a.m. If that's true, he left sometime between four a.m. and eight a.m."

Aunt Pearl scoffed. "Like she's going to tell the truth. Sheesh."

"You got anything better?"

"I guess not," Aunt Pearl admitted.

Mom frowned. "How could Tonya possibly not notice him missing? Their suite door squeaks." Even with our extensive renovations, there were still a few squeaks and creaks around. "He couldn't get out of bed without her noticing. That guy's morbidly obese."

"She claims she took a sleeping pill and was completely knocked out," I said.

Aunt Pearl rolled her eyes. "Likely story."

"Maybe she was asleep, or maybe she's lying. We need someone to corroborate her story," I said. "Do you know something different?"

"She was sleeping all right. Just not alone."

Another bombshell from Aunt Pearl. Her information with-holding made me fear the worst. "You snuck into their room? How could you invade their privacy like that?"

"Relax, Cen. I did nothing of the sort." Aunt Pearl smirked. "I had help."

"Grandma Vi!" I was both angry and pleased that Aunt Pearl had enlisted Grandma Vi's help. Angry at the gross violation of privacy, but pleased that Grandma Vi's incognito visit resulted in a new lead. As long as Aunt Pearl was telling the truth, that is.

Aunt Pearl nodded. "Your grandma was bored out of her mind in that messy tree house of yours, so she dropped by for a visit."

I was miffed by her housekeeping reference, but also annoyed at Grandma Vi's secret late night escapades. "Who was in Tonya's room with her?"

"Did I say she was in her own room?"

"Pearl, cut to the chase." Mom had reached the end of her rope too. "Where was Tonya and who was she with?"

My head spun. Our dozen guest rooms were all occupied. Tonya must have paired up with another guest, but who? An affair, a trou-bled marriage, and ruthless ambitions just increased Tonya's motive for murder. Yet Aunt Pearl was certain that the killer in the gazebo was a man, not a woman.

"She was with a man who was not her husband." Aunt Pearl hummed theme music from a television game show. "Any guesses?"

I rolled my eyes as I turned to my aunt. "Give us a straight answer for once."

"I'm kind of enjoying myself," Aunt Pearl said. "But clearly you're not, so I'll tell you. Tonya was in another man's room. And they weren't doing a lot of talking, if you catch my drift."

"They were having sex while Sebastien was in the gazebo?" I gasped, unable to believe I was having this conversation with my mom and aunt. Then again, I never would have expected any of this twenty-four hours ago.

"Don't play games, Pearl," Mom said. "We've got a murder on our grand opening, and you're the prime suspect. If you know something, you need to speak up now."

"Especially if it differs from Tonya's own account." I cracked open the door to the dining room and peered out. Tyler Gates still sat with Tonya Plant. He was taking copious notes, writing furiously. I would give a stack of pancakes to see what he was writing down in his notebook. "Quick, Aunt Pearl, catch him before he leaves."

Aunt Pearl crossed her arms. "I am not talking to that man."

"Forget about the fine," I said. "You're pretty much the only suspect now. It will only get worse unless you tell him what you know. This isn't the time for petty differences."

"A five-hundred-dollar fine is hardly petty. I'll need to take in extra students to make ends meet."

I wanted to add that she deserved every penny of that fine, but escalating the dispute made matters worse. "You won't have any students if you're convicted of murder."

"Who would do something like this? Why frame Pearl?" Mom shook her head. "This could be the death of our town too."

"All she has to do is tell the sheriff everything and she can clear herself." I looked pointedly at my aunt. Mom had a blind spot when it came to her sister. She considered Pearl victimized rather than reckless and irresponsible.

"Stop being so dramatic, Ruby. You're like everyone else in this town—always overreacting." Aunt Pearl shook her head.

I threw my arms up in the air. "Talk about overreacting. You're the pyromaniac setting fire to our very own gazebo. You sabotage everything just to get what you want. Maybe you want to erase our town off the map by burning down the highway sign, but other people matter too. If I didn't know you better, I'd suspect you just like the sheriff does." He hadn't exactly called her a suspect, but I had to scare Aunt Pearl straight. Her shenanigans and information withholding ruined our chances of success and jeopardized the whole town's future.

Mom's mouth dropped open in shock at my tirade. Maybe I had overdone it, but Aunt Pearl's attention-getting antics and lack of cooperation frustrated me.

"I can't imagine someone like Tonya would—or could—murder her husband. We can't just accuse her without proof," Mom said. "I actually feel sorry for her. We invited her and Sebastien here, and now he's been murdered. It's our fault in a way. We should be nice to her."

"But what about Tonya's breakfast potion?" I thought Mom's sympathy was misplaced, since Tonya had plans to bewitch us.

Mom frowned. "What potion?"

"Cen's confused." Aunt Pearl clamped a bony hand on my shoulder.

I started to protest but Aunt Pearl only gripped tighter. By now I realized that her claim against Tonya was another fabrication. Mom knew nothing about Tonya's purported potion to render us powerless. Mom probably had no idea Hazel was here either.

I glared at Aunt Pearl.

Aunt Pearl scowled. "You're so blind to people's motives, Ruby. Wake up. Tonya's guilty. Everything started with that stupid highway sign. It has to go."

"Your Charm School customers don't need a highway sign, but tourists do," I said. "They inject cash into our little economy. Your students hardly spend a dime." Witches were notoriously cheap. Why spend cash for something you could conjure up?

Mom stepped between us. "Now, now, ladies. Be civil to one another. Fighting gets us nowhere." She turned to me. "Cen, you don't think the Sheriff really suspects Pearl, do you? He must have other leads."

I shrugged. "She has a motive. She doesn't want tourism. She made that very clear with the burning of the sign. And she refuses to cooperate. Mostly it's because of her wand in the gazebo, though."

Aunt Pearl obviously hadn't told Mom about Hazel's visit and her suspicions about Tonya either. That bothered me. "Aunt Pearl looks suspicious until we find the real killer."

Mom shook her head. "I wish you wouldn't act out so much, Pearl. There's no reason we can't all coexist. You can still operate Pearl's Charm School, but you have to do it discreetly. Can you do that?"

Pearl nodded slowly.

While Aunt Pearl always tried to keep her youngest sister in the dark, she did listen to her.

"Now would be a good time to go up to Tonya's room and freshen it up." Mom patted Pearl's shoulder. "Some flowers would be a nice touch."

That sounded like a terrible idea to me, but I knew Mom was just trying to keep Pearl occupied. It surprised me that Mom didn't seem to know Tonya was a witch, but I didn't dare say anything. Things could deteriorate quickly and I didn't want to tempt fate.

# CHAPTER 24

*I* got so distracted thinking about Grandma Vi's sleuthing and Tonya's mystery man that I completely forgot about Tonya's fruit plate. I assembled a generous assortment of grapes, cantaloupe, and honeydew melon along with some cheese and headed back out into the dining room.

Tonya Plant smiled as I approached. Her serene expression seemed misplaced considering her recent loss. She stopped mid-sentence as I approached the table and put the plate down in front of her.

"Thank you, Cendrine," said Sheriff Gates. "That will be all."

I nodded and stepped away a few feet to the next table, where I busied myself adjusting the tableware place settings. I waited for Tonya to resume speaking but she didn't. I quickly ran out of things to do.

I felt eyes bore into me, and I turned to see Sheriff Gates glaring at me. I moved to the next table.

Tonya resumed speaking, but her voice was so soft I had to strain my ears to hear anything. I dropped a fork on the floor and jumped as it jangled.

Tonya paused mid-sentence as I picked up the fork. As I straightened I looked up and met the angry eyes of Tonya Plant.

Sheriff Gates turned in his seat. They both glared at me.

"What?"

"Can you give us a bit of privacy, Cendrine?" Tyler Gates tilted his head towards the kitchen.

"Uh yeah, sorry." I retreated to the counter and refilled my coffee cup. I was too far away to hear anything more than a few snippets of conversation. Tonya claimed to have checked in very early Friday morning, which corroborated Aunt Pearl's version of events, though she said she had forgotten the exact time. Finally we were getting at the truth.

I couldn't see the sheriff's expression, so I had no idea if he believed Tonya or not. It was essential that I get Tonya's accounting of what happened. The sheriff was dealing with a witch and didn't know it, so he needed my help. It was the only way to validate or disprove her claims and to get at the truth.

I brightened as I realized I could refill the condiments. I grabbed the salt and pepper containers and returned to the table behind the sheriff. I walked softly and avoided eye contact with Tonya. I hoped she would continue with her story and not signal to the sheriff that I was right behind him.

"Seb wanted to go for a walk," Tonya said. "But I was tired, so I told him to go ahead without me."

*At four o'clock in the morning? Likely story.*

"What time was this?" Sheriff Gates leaned back in his chair and clasped his hands behind his head.

I froze. His arms were just inches from me and had the effect of trapping me in between his chair and my table. I sucked in my breath and tried not to make any noise. If Tonya took any notice, it wasn't apparent as she just kept talking.

"Around eight or nine a.m., I think. I had taken a sleeping pill around that time, so I was dozing off." Tonya's voice was strong and clear, not the soft and broken whisper of a bereaved widow.

"And you slept till when?"

"I don't know...around three or so. I woke shortly before you came to my room."

"And you saw no one during this time?"

"No."

According to Grandma Vi, Tonya had been with another man from around lunchtime onward. Assuming Grandma's timeline was correct, the sheriff had just caught Tonya in a lie. Only he'd never know it, unless I found a way to disprove Tonya's story. I needed to find this man. I also needed to find the gloves on the Walmart receipt. The antifreeze container was important too, but I might already have liquid proof in the Gatorade bottle. I was lost in thought, oblivious to the fact that I had turned around until my eyes locked on Sheriff Gates.

He turned around in his seat and faced me. "You can't stay here while I'm questioning Mrs. Plant, Cendrine." His warm brown eyes locked on mine.

"I can't exactly go anywhere. You're in my restaurant. I work here."

The sheriff stood and waved me away as Tonya gave me a cold, hard stare. I felt a stab of fear. I couldn't give him the receipt in front of her, but it didn't seem like Tyler Gates was leaving anytime soon. The longer he stayed, the greater the delay before I could pass on my new lead. The sheriff was at a terrible disadvantage without help from someone with the complete picture. That someone was me.

* * *

I WATCHED from the kitchen doorway as Sheriff Gates resumed his seat opposite Tonya Plant. I super-tuned my ear until I reached a volume adequate to pick up snippets of their conversation. If she was as manipulative as Hazel and Aunt Pearl claimed, I had no choice but to use my magic to listen to discover what Tonya was up to. It hadn't even occurred to me to use magic to amplify my

134

hearing. Once I thought of it, it took me several more minutes because I was so rusty I had forgotten half the spell. If only I had thought to use my magic earlier. I could have been much more discreet.

"Cendrine!"

I just about jumped out of my skin. "You scared the crap out of me! Why are you yelling at me like that?"

Aunt Pearl frowned. "I wasn't yelling at all. You wouldn't be using your extrasensory powers on the Sheriff, now would you?"

She had caught me red-handed. "This is an emergency."

"How is your emergency different from my emergencies?" Aunt Pearl crossed her arms. "You call me a troublemaker. Look at you, little miss by-the-books. It's fine for you to use your magic, but it's not okay for me?"

"These are extenuating circumstances, Aunt Pearl."

Mom turned around at the grill. "Are you eavesdropping?"

"Of course not," I said.

"Yes she is," Aunt Pearl said.

"Only to help you, because you won't help yourself," I said.

Mom shook her head. "Didn't we agree there would be no magic within range of the guests?"

"I have no choice. Aunt Pearl is one of the primary suspects because of her pyromaniac tendencies."

Mom rolled her eyes. "You're not bringing up the highway sign again. Honestly, Cendrine, you're like a dog with a bone. You just never let up."

"Ruby's right," Aunt Pearl said. "You're always picking on me. Show your elders some respect."

I threw my hands up, exasperated. "While we're bickering, Tonya's scheming how to ruin our town. She not only gets rid of her husband but also the guy that would have put Westwick Corners on the map. She killed him, I'm sure of it. But everything that's happened so far incriminates Aunt Pearl." I turned to my aunt. "She's trying to frame you."

Mom's mouth dropped open. "They can't possibly think that Pearl—"

Pearl stomped her feet. "I'm a witch, for crying out loud. I don't have to murder anyone. There are far easier ways to get rid of someone."

"The sheriff doesn't know that. He doesn't know the first thing about witches, vortexes, or any of that stuff. Now do you see my point?" I turned my attention back to Tonya Plant and the sheriff.

"Tell the sheriff what you know, Pearl." Mom's voice rose and I could tell she was getting upset.

"I'll think about it," Pearl said. "But first I've got some cleaning to do." She turned and left before we could stop her.

I didn't think for a minute Aunt Pearl was the culprit, but she was doing a pretty good job of acting like one.

Aunt Pearl had said that Tonya had been with another man, but she refused to say who. If she wouldn't tell me, there were other ways to find out.

# CHAPTER 25

*I* couldn't eavesdrop unnoticed anymore on Tonya Plant and the sheriff but I could find out more about the man she was spending time with. I headed to the front desk and pulled out the guest register.

Almost all of the dozen guest rooms were occupied by couples except for three. One room was occupied by two women and another had a single woman. The third room was occupied by one Jack Tupper III. It was a stroke of luck to find only one room with a single male guest. It was a bit of a leap to rule out any of the attached men, but I had a hunch that Jack was our man.

My pulse quickened when I saw the room number.

It was Grandma Vi's old room. The very room she claimed to have seen Tonya together with the mystery man.

Well, it was a mystery no more.

Tonya's secret man was almost certainly Jack Tupper III.

I didn't recognize his pretentious-sounding name, but it was enough to uncover more about him and his whereabouts at the time of the murder. I closed the register, pleased with my find.

If Pearl's claims of their tryst were true, Jack almost certainly knew Tonya prior to visiting the Inn. In fact, he probably followed her here. Maybe he was the hooded man from the gazebo.

Once I uncovered his and Tonya's relationship, I could bring the connection to the sheriff's attention without being obvious. Tonya would almost certainly deny an affair, and I couldn't exactly tell the sheriff that ghostly Grandma Vi had been stalking them. But there were bound to be things the sheriff could find, like cell phone records and such. All I had to do was come up with leads to steer the investigation away from Aunt Pearl and onto evidence that pointed to the real killer.

I headed back into the dining room, eager to share my find with Mom. I reached the doorway and stopped in my tracks as I stared at the full dining room. Brayden sat a few tables away from the sheriff and Tonya Plant. I dreaded having "the talk" with him, but I needed to do it soon. Seeing him just reminded me of that. I wasn't looking forward to it. Calling off the wedding was huge, and we would probably break up over it.

Whether I wanted that or not, I wasn't even sure right now. In fact, I was no longer sure about anything. I didn't know if I still loved him, or whether I really ever had. He was my first and only boyfriend, and until now I had never really thought of a future without him. Everything had just kind of seemed preordained.

Thankfully Brayden wasn't alone, so I could procrastinate a little longer. A man with unnatural-looking reddish-blond shoulder-length hair sat opposite Brayden with his back to me. It was almost certainly the man from last night in the vineyard. It had been dark, but the man had the same slim, athletic build.

Brayden caught my eye immediately and smiled. He waved me over. "Cen, this is my friend Jack. He's from Shady Creek, and he's staying here." He motioned to the tanned, thirty-something man across the table. "Jack, this is Cen. Her family owns the place."

I was speechless as my brain synapses took control. This must be the same Jack who was staying in Grandma Vi's old room.

Jack stood and shook my right hand with his left, pointing

apologetically to his bandaged right hand. He was slightly taller than Brayden and a few years older, with an aura of superiority about him. "Quaint little place you got here. When are you doing your renovations? It'll look great with a face lift."

"It's just fine the way it is," I growled at his intentional insult. Even if Brayden hadn't told him of our grand opening, it was plastered all over the building. As a guest he had to be aware of it.

Brayden shot me a warning look.

I glared at both of them as my stomach growled to remind me that I needed food.

"If you like that sort of look." Jack tossed his head back and laughed. His perfectly styled hair didn't move an inch. He pulled a business card from his shirt pocket and handed it to me. "Give me a call if you're interested in selling the place. I'll be honest, though. This place is a teardown, so the only value is in the land. Lucky for you though, we're always looking for large properties like yours."

The card read *Jack Tupper III, Senior Vice-President, Development, Centralex.*

My mouth dropped open as I connected Jack, the plans in Tonya's suite, and the late night vineyard business. Maybe the biggest realization was that Brayden hadn't been straight with me.

"We're not interested in selling." I wanted to run into the kitchen and tell Mom everything. That didn't help though, so I willed myself to remain calm and get as much information as I could. Jack was obviously Tonya's co-conspirator and apparently her lover too.

Jack shook his head. "Your business won't survive once my new resort, conference center, and mall opens. And casino. The only reason you get business now is because you're the only place in town."

My face flushed as I fought to control my temper. The guy had a lot of nerve telling me that our business was doomed at the very moment he chomped down on Mom's breakfast special. I also knew from the plans in Tonya's room that Centralex intended to build on our property, not anywhere else. Jack was using scare tactics to get our property at a cheap price. Well, we weren't going to be intimidated. Not if I could help it.

Brayden cleared his throat. "Jack's plans include a resort hotel."

My face reddened. Brayden was wheeling and dealing again, only this time for a business in direct competition with ours. "But we just opened the Inn. Westwick Corners isn't big enough to support another hotel." Brayden's job as mayor was to encourage business and commerce, but that didn't mean getting chummy with the developer. He hadn't given the Westwick Corners Inn much support, despite his part-time job at *The Witching Post*. What favors did he expect from Jack?

"This is big, Cen. The resort will have two hundred rooms, along with a conference center. A destination resort, not just a little boutique operation. It will put Westwick Corners on the map."

It was as if someone had stabbed me in the back. Our property had been in our family for generations and Brayden knew we'd never sell come hell or high water. He also knew we had no other means of earning a living. Yet he'd been aligning with an out-of-town developer and even scoping our property by moonlight with Jack. He had purposely timed their excursion during the cover of night to avoid detection. What else wasn't he telling me?

My face flushed as anger welled inside me. I was about to lose it. "I've got to go." I turned on my heels.

Jack called after me. "I'm doing you a favor, but my offer is only good till Monday."

"We aren't selling," I repeated. "We've just started our business."

"There's definitely money to be made, Cen," Brayden yelled after me.

I shook my head and kept walking.

Brayden suddenly appeared at my side. He squeezed my arm. "I'll stop by your place later this morning, Cen. We'll catch up."

"Uh...I'm a little busy right now. I'll call you later." I took a deep breath and headed for the kitchen. I debated whether to tell Mom about Jack's proposal now or after breakfast. It was bound to upset her, but she needed to know.

Mom, Aunt Pearl, and Aunt Amber owned the place together. It was even more insulting that Jack hadn't approached any of them directly. He had told me on purpose, of course. My second-hand information would soften the blow that an outsider planned to compete with us. But after seeing the Centralex development plans in Tonya's room, I knew that wasn't the intent at all. Jack's real goal was to steal our land out from under us and bulldoze our beautiful historic mansion to the ground.

I swore under my breath as everything became crystal clear. Aunt Pearl's outlandish vortex claims were 100% true. Tonya had already partnered with the biggest developer around, and getting our land was just a formality.

Money had a way of making people do crazy things. Grandma Vi was right not only about the property but also about Brayden. He had placed his business interests ahead of my family's livelihood.

I was halfway to the kitchen when chairs scraped against hardwood in the direction of Sheriff Gates' and Tonya's table. I spun around as they stood. I guessed that he had finished with Tonya for now. I reversed and headed towards him, but Brayden intercepted me.

"Cen, wait." Brayden strode towards me, plate in hand. His cutlery clattered on his plateful of eggs and toast as he caught up to me. "You seem mad or something."

"I saw you last night in the vineyard with Jack," I said as we walked side-by-side towards the kitchen. "I didn't know your mayoral duties extended to secretly showing our place to property developers."

"It's not like that at all, Cen. You're jumping to conclusions."

"Then why were you sneaking around in the middle of the night? You're obsessed with our property all of a sudden."

"I am not obsessed and we weren't sneaking around." Brayden's voice rose as we neared the kitchen door. "Jack just likes to keep a low profile. If he shows too much interest, prices skyrocket."

"So it is about getting our land." I stopped just outside the door and faced him. "You tell your friend Jack that our land isn't for sale."

"You're making a big deal, as usual, Cen." Brayden rolled his eyes and turned. "I've got to go. Well discuss this later."

"Oh, and Brayden?"

"Yeah?" Brayden stopped but didn't even turn to face me.

"The wedding's off."

Brayden spun around and stared in open-mouthed shock. Then, for the first time in a long while, he listened to me.

# CHAPTER 26

*B*rayden sat at the small bistro table just inside the kitchen entrance. It was stacked with dishes and restaurant supplies, but he cleared a space for his plate and resumed eating. He speared a potato wedge on his fork and twirled it in his ketchup. "What's gotten into you, Cen?" His mouth turned down into a pout, designed to get my pity. It didn't work. I was too mad this time.

"Nothing's gotten into me." I wasn't about to have an outburst in Mom's kitchen within earshot of other people. "Something has taken hold of you though. Whatever it is, I don't like it."

Brayden's eyes narrowed as he studied me. "Something is very different about you. You're so negative all of a sudden. You're stressed with all the wedding planning." He patted my shoulder like I was a child.

"You're absolutely right," I said. "This wedding thing is too rushed, so I'm calling it off. With everything that's happened, I'm having second thoughts."

Brayden bit his lip. "We've been dating for years, Cen. How can you possibly think the wedding is rushed?"

"Something just doesn't feel right. I need some time to myself to think about things."

"We don't have the luxury of time. You should have done all your thinking a year ago when you said yes."

"A lot has changed since then." My realization that Brayden's political aspirations always came before me, for instance. Our wedding was a tick box on his to-do list. I, like everyone else, had just assumed we would marry. I had never even given it a second thought until now, probably because I was afraid to face the truth.

"Like what?"

"You wouldn't understand." My attraction to Tyler Gates was just infatuation, but it was a very real symptom of my unhappiness with Brayden. While I could do rewind spells, I couldn't rewind my life. Once I chose my path with Brayden, there was no going back. It had taken a murder at my wedding rehearsal to stop and take stock of my life.

Brayden stood. "Don't do this to me, Cen. We've got two hundred guests coming, including the governor. You can't cancel now." He shook his head slowly. "Do you know how this will look?"

"I don't care what the governor or anyone else thinks. I just can't go through with it." I did care what my family thought though. Especially Mom, who had worked so hard on every detail. I hated to disappoint her.

"You're just emotional because of the murder and everything." He placed an arm around my shoulder. "Look, I know I should have been at the rehearsal, but I got caught up with work. I promise I'll make it better."

"Sheriff Gates told me your Crime Watch meeting got canceled. You weren't even at a meeting, yet you couldn't be bothered to come to the rehearsal. If I'm not worth your time, why should I marry you?"

"That's just not fair, Cen. The meeting was canceled because of a scheduling conflict. That's the truth. Jack only had one hour free in the afternoon, so my schedule got rearranged a bit."

"Is that so?" My sense of indignation grew. "No doubt you were talking about getting him some cheap land."

Anger flashed in Brayden's eyes. "You should be grateful I got him interested in our town. Centralex is the best thing that's happened to Westwick Corners in a long, long time."

I fumed as I recalled Brayden's late night pacing outside my tree house. It was all I could do to keep my voice calm. "No one's selling, including us. There's nothing else for sale in town, and everything else is farmland."

"You'd be surprised, Cen. Anyone will sell if the price is right."

"Anyone?" I raised my brows. "Shady Creek didn't bite."

Brayden scraped egg yolk off his plate with his fork. "The Westwick Corners Inn is too small-scale to make any money. Your family will just bankrupt itself. The smart thing is to sell, because offers like Jack's don't come along every day. At least listen to him and see what he has to say."

My face flushed. "We're not selling, especially after fixing everything up. You should know that. You sound like you're in business with Jack yourself."

"Don't be ridiculous. It's my job as mayor to look at new opportunities. I'm working to get what we all want for Westwick Corners —jobs and growth."

"We don't want it at any cost." Brayden had sold us out. Our town councillors were all over seventy and basically voted however Brayden did, so Jack would get what he wanted, one way or another. "Why did Shady Creek reject his plans?"

"Traffic issues." Brayden laughed. "Can you believe that? Who doesn't want more traffic?"

I knew of at least one person, and she would certainly take action.

"We'll talk more once you've had a chance to cool down."

His dismissive attitude really irritated me. "There's nothing more to talk about. It's over."

Brayden's mouth dropped open as he stared at me, speechless.

He waited for me to say more, but I was done. After a minute he turned to go, then turned back and grabbed his half-eaten breakfast before he exited and slammed the door behind him.

# CHAPTER 27

*I* sat at the bistro table for a few more minutes, mostly to be sure Brayden and Jack were both gone from the dining room. I didn't hear any noise or conversation coming from the dining room, so I crept to the door and peeked outside.

I breathed a sigh of relief as I scanned the almost empty dining room. Jack was gone, and so were the other guests. No one had heard me arguing with Brayden. I opened the door a crack further and my heart sank as I spotted Tyler Gates over at a table by the window, alone.

He caught the door's motion and met my gaze. Our eyes remained locked for a split second before he turned away. He knew.

Great.

The one person I hadn't wanted to know about my troubled relationship had obviously heard everything. I turned around and walked back into the kitchen, deflated.

How awkward.

I wanted to talk to him about the case, and this just made me want to avoid him. But Aunt Pearl needed help fast, so I couldn't exactly hide under a rock.

"You did the right thing."

I jumped at the voice behind me, not expecting anyone else in the kitchen. "Huh?"

Grandma Vi floated a few feet away from me in a purpley haze.

"You promised to stay at the tree house, Grandma."

"I can't stay away when I'm needed. Brayden's all wrong for you. It'll take a few days but it will all blow over."

"Of course you think that. You never liked him in the first place." I sat back down at the table, deflated at the prospect of canceling the wedding. "How am I going to un-invite two hundred people?"

"We'll figure out a way." Grandma Vi sat down—or rather hovered—opposite me. "Now you can make a play for that handsome new sheriff."

"I'll do no such thing. All my energies are focused on solving Sebastien Plant's murder and clearing Aunt Pearl. Tell me what you know about Tonya Plant and Jack Tupper."

"Who's Jack?" Grandma Vi asked.

"The one sneaking around with Brayden last night," I said.

"The one in my room."

"It's not your—" I stopped myself mid-sentence. No point in upsetting Grandma more. I took a deep breath. "We all agreed to open the Inn and we've all made sacrifices. You can't spy on people like that."

"I was homesick. And Pearl promised not to tell anyone." Grandma Vi frowned. "Pearl never could keep a secret."

"I made her tell me," I said. "She's about to get charged with Plant's murder unless we do something about it. What did Tonya and Jack talk about when you were there?"

"There wasn't much talking going on in that room. Tonya's husband isn't even in the ground yet and that scoundrel's making out with her."

"It takes two to tango."

Grandma Vi sighed. "They can't just steal our land out from under us, can they?"

"Not unless we agree to sell it, and we're not going to do that."

"They seem to think it's already theirs," Grandma Vi said. "Tonya's playing that Jack guy, though. He's too lovesick to see it."

I couldn't imagine abrasive Jack being lovesick, but maybe he was different behind closed doors. "I need your help to solve the murder, Grandma. I want you to follow Tonya everywhere she goes."

"You mean like, spy on her? I thought that wasn't allowed."

"In this case, it is." We couldn't leave her unguarded for a moment. Grandma Vi wouldn't stay at my place no matter what I did, so I might as well use her talents.

"But she's a witch. She'll see me," Grandma Vi said. "Why don't I spy on Jack instead?"

I shook my head. "I'll watch him. I need someone powerful against Tonya, and your magic is much better than mine."

That seemed to appease her. "Under one condition."

I sighed. "Fine, name it." Why did every promise in my family come with conditions attached?

"I want my old room back."

I nodded. One way or another, we all wanted something back. I just wasn't so sure if we would get what we wanted with no strings attached.

# CHAPTER 28

$\mathcal{I}$ opened the kitchen back door, feeling terribly guilty about Brayden. While I was furious at him, I probably could have picked a better time to vent my anger, not to mention call off the wedding.

I debated running after Brayden, but he was already halfway to the parking lot where Jack had just climbed into the driver's seat of a red Lamborghini. Maybe it was better to leave him alone while everything sunk in, but I already felt so guilty for hurting him. I didn't want to take back my words in a moment of weakness, but he had every right to be upset.

On the other hand, Brayden no longer seemed all that upset. He shouted to catch Jack's attention.

Jack leaned out his window and said something I couldn't make out.

Brayden laughed. He watched as Jack's car peeled out of the parking lot and disappeared down the hill.

I sighed and turned back towards the door. I knew I should tell Mom about Jack's limited offer, but it just depressed me. It would depress her too and I wasn't ready to deal with more upset. It bothered me to no end that Jack had the nerve to eat and stay at the Westwick Corners Inn at the very moment he was planning to destroy it.

But Jack's hypocrisy and his temporary absence provided a small window of opportunity. I could sneak into his room and see if I could glean any more information on the development.

I ran up the stairs and paused on the landing. I drew in my breath, shocked that I had pretty much turned into Aunt Pearl. Maybe her blend of ornery insanity was hereditary.

I bounded up the last flight of stairs thinking that if our business wasn't sunk already, our reputation would soon be. We were doomed if customers discovered that the staff rifled through their rooms while they ate breakfast.

No, I wasn't Aunt Pearl. I also had a perfectly good reason to check for soap and shampoo supplies. I headed down the hall, stopping at the supply room for a handful of toiletries. My spirits lifted at the chance to do something productive for a change.

The hallway was empty when I unlocked Jack's door. His room was a mess, with bedsheets and towels strewn all over the floor. I entered the bathroom and was alarmed to see bloodstains in the bathtub. I got over my initial shock and realized it probably came from his bandaged hand.

But how had he hurt his hand in the first place?

I flashed back to my aunt and her fear of blood. There was no way she could have checked out the bathroom without freaking out.

I studied the room. Aside from the blood, nothing else seemed out of the ordinary in the bathroom, but something immediately caught my eye in the trash can by the desk. A bloody tire iron sat in the trash can. Jack hardly seemed the sort to self-mutilate, let alone with a tire iron.

Suddenly everything made sense. A tire iron was enough to kill anyone, including a large man like Sebastien Plant. Plant just happened to be Jack's romantic rival. Jack was both tall enough and strong enough to deliver a lethal blow to Sebastien Plant. And a drunk Sebastien Plant wouldn't put up much of a fight.

I spun around and headed towards the door. I had to tell the sheriff immediately so he could cordon off the room and gather evidence. Jack obviously hadn't expected anyone in his room. He had temporarily left the tire iron in the trash can until he could dispose of it after dark.

My heart stopped as I ran smack into Grandma Vi. She must have covertly followed me.

"You scared me half to death, Cen!" She floated to a corner above the door and regarded me with a smirk.

"You're already dead, Grandma. Why did you follow me to Jack's room?"

"It's my room, not Jack's, and I'll come in here whenever I please." She cast a disapproving glance around the room. "This is a disgrace. He's even messier than you are."

I ignored her insult. "Grandma, please. You can't sneak around the guests' rooms like this."

"Why not? You're exploring too."

"No, I'm not. I just came to drop off some shampoo and stuff." I showed her my handful of mini soaps and shampoo bottles.

"Nice try, missy. Don't forget that I can read your mind. If you're so suspicious of this Jack guy, why don't you let me help?"

"No, Grandma. I've got to go know. I need to let the sheriff know about the tire iron." I headed towards the door and froze in my tracks as a key turned in the lock.

152

# CHAPTER 29

"*W*hat the hell are you doing in my room?" Jack Tupper III's form filled the doorway and blocked the sunlight that streamed in from the hallway. He also blocked my exit.

"Housekeeping. Just dropping off some toiletries." My face flushed as I lamely held up my hand. It was painfully obvious that I was nowhere near the bathroom. I hadn't even anticipated that Jack might return. He must have forgotten something.

"No need." He waved his hand towards the doorway. "I think you'd better go."

I lurched towards the door, dropping the shampoo and soap on the bureau as I brushed past him.

I slammed the door behind me and didn't look back.

I raced down the stairs, into the dining room and straight to Sheriff Gates' table. I noticed with dismay that Tonya was seated again. I simply couldn't wait any longer. "I need to talk to you."

Tonya Plant's eyes narrowed as they locked on mine.

She knew I was on to something. I felt a sudden stab of fear as I recalled Hazel and Pearl's warning. I should have waited until the sheriff was alone, but under the circumstances, how could I? Jack was probably getting rid of the tire iron right now.

"What is it?" He seemed to notice my anxiety.

"It's confidential." I glanced at Tonya, who by now was on high alert. That only meant one thing to me. She was involved in her husband's murder and suspected I was about to talk about it. What else could be urgent enough to interrupt the sheriff's interview? "Can we talk in the kitchen?"

He glanced at Tonya, who nodded. "Give me five minutes."

* * *

TEN MINUTES later Tyler Gates faced me across the kitchen bistro table.

He leaned forward and spoke in a low voice. "This is all confidential, but a tire iron fits better with the coroner's findings."

"Should you be telling all me this? Don't forget that I'm the press."

"Telling you is part of my strategy. I'm hoping you can publish a story that will flush out the real killers. Somebody in town knows something."

"SO YOU'RE RULING out Aunt Pearl and her cane?"

He shook his head. "Nothing and nobody is ruled out, but it was obvious to me that the cane wasn't heavy enough to do the kind of damage we saw on Plant's skull."

I shuddered. "You'd better hurry before Jack destroys the evidence." He had been awfully careless—or maybe overconfident—to simply throw the tire iron in the trash can. Whoever cleaned the room—meaning Aunt Pearl, the very person being framed—was certain to notice it. But apparently Jack thought we were all too stupid to make the connection. Or maybe he hadn't had time to dispose of it.

154

"The crime scene techs are on their way back from Shady Creek," Tyler said. "I called them back when I came in here."

"Tonya didn't hear you, I hope."

"No, she left in a hurry just after you."

Great. I had to alert Aunt Pearl and Hazel that Tonya was on to us. "Is she a suspect? She is the spouse, after all. She doesn't seem too heartbroken if you ask me."

"Everyone's a suspect until the case is solved," he said.

"She's involved somehow. You know about their affair?"

His eyes widened. "We're on it. The question is how do you know about their relationship?"

I fidgeted as I thought up an excuse. I couldn't mention that my ghost grandma had staked out Jack's room. "We saw Tonya sneaking into Jack's room."

"And you think that is proof enough of their affair? You've got to have more than that."

I did have more but nothing I could tell him. "Tonya and Jack are business partners. Jack's trying to scare us into selling our land to build a Travel Unraveled resort. Sebastien was against the idea. I think that's why they killed him."

The sheriff fell silent while he digested my statement. I got the sense he was debating how much to tell me.

"There's more." I pulled the Walmart receipt from my pocket and handed it to him as I described the Gatorade bottle in the trash. "I don't think he was drunk. Tonya poisoned him with antifreeze but then got Jack to hit him with the tire iron. When he died from the poison, she could still pin the murder on Jack." The scapegoat idea came to me as I spoke. It made perfect sense that Tonya would frame Jack. That way she could keep all the spoils for herself.

In my sensory-deprived hungry state, everything came together with a shocking clarity that had escaped me until now.

Tyler Gates nodded. "That ties in with the coroner's report. Sebastien Plant was subject to a lot of blunt force trauma, exactly the type of injuries you would get from a tire iron. But strangely enough, he didn't bleed as much as he should have."

"You mean he might have already been dead when he was hit?" I remembered seeing something similar on *Forensic Files.*

His eyes widened in surprise. "Yes."

I flashed back to the Gatorade bottle in Tonya's room. "Did the autopsy show signs of poisoning?"

Tyler's eyes clouded over as he picked up his phone and punched in some numbers. "That's exactly what we need to find out."

# CHAPTER 30

estwick Corners' single jail cell didn't see a lot of action. The cell was occupied on rare occasions by drunken revelers but never, as far as I knew, by a witch. Today's guest of honor was Aunt Pearl. She had been caught red-handed with her wand—or cane—as the sheriff believed it to be. He had followed her to the gas station after seeing her with another gas can. He confiscated it in order to prevent further pyromania. He also took her wand. Getting gas wasn't exactly illegal, but stealing police evidence was.

The sheriff's details were fuzzy, but somehow Aunt Pearl had gotten away. I had no doubt her magic played a part in both his memory loss and her reunion with her wand from the police evidence locker. I promised to bring her in to face justice.

One thing I couldn't explain was how she had stolen her wand—or cane—in the first place. The lock was intact, with no signs of tampering.

The only good that came of Aunt Pearl's antics was that she finally agreed to accompany me to the police station to come clean. I feared she would try to steal her wand again, but it was a chance I had to take. I convinced her that the sheriff would keep watching her unless she provided information to generate new leads. To my surprise, she agreed. Both of us knew that would include uncomfortable questions about her wand. Her behavior so far just created confusion and incriminated her, and I really hoped she would just cooperate.

Aunt Pearl hadn't been formally charged yet, but a part of me thought a jail cell was the safest possible place for her. As a witch she could bust out anytime she wanted, but that only made things worse for her. I needed to convince her to stay put while I got the goods on Tonya. Anything less just played into Tonya's master plan to frame Aunt Pearl. I had no proof of any of this, just a gut feeling and the knowledge that no one in my family, including Aunt Pearl, was a murderer.

Another part of me wondered why Sheriff Gates had locked up Aunt Pearl rather than focusing on the evidence incriminating Tonya and Jack. The law operated on cold, hard facts, and I had finally found proof that pointed away from Aunt Pearl. The sheriff had plenty of reasons to haul those two in for questioning, but he had already used up the one cell available to him. I hoped he knew what he was doing.

Grandma Vi's plan for Aunt Pearl to tail Tonya had fizzled pretty quickly with Aunt Pearl in custody, so we were back to square one. I had arrived at the station minutes after Sheriff Gates' call, accompanied by Grandma Vi.

After several unsuccessful attempts to convince Grandma Vi to look for Tonya, I gave up. I understood Grandma Vi's priorities. Aunt Pearl might be seventy years old, but Pearl was still Grandma Vi's daughter. Her maternal instincts had kicked in.

"We've got to spring her out of this joint, Cen."

"Relax, Grandma. I think she's just here for questioning." Deep down I worried that the sheriff hadn't explained exactly why Aunt Pearl was in custody. Knowing Aunt Pearl, it could be any number of things. Suddenly arson seemed pretty minor compared to murder. I worried that she had taken things too far.

We waited in the small reception area of the office that served as Westwick Corners police station. A half dozen vinyl-backed chairs lined one wall of the reception area and faced a wood-paneled counter that dated back to the last city hall reno in the 1970s. I picked up a two-year-old *Time* magazine and flipped through the ragged pages, but I couldn't concentrate.

The police station was housed on the first floor of city hall. It was the last place I wanted to be right now. The mayor's office was in the same building and I dreaded crossing paths with Brayden.

Grandma Vi paced, or rather floated, back and forth across the waiting room and in and out of the interview room that housed Sheriff Gates and Aunt Pearl.

"Would you stop? You're frantic floating is giving me a headache."

"I can't help it, Cen. It doesn't look good for Pearl. He's really grilling her." Grandma Vi hovered above me, her apparition lighter than usual due to the emotional distress of her daughter being questioned.

The voices coming from the sheriff's private office were muted, but I was pretty sure they belonged to Tyler Gates and Aunt Pearl. No one else was here.

"You only heard snippets of conversation. Maybe you misinter-preted something." I was annoyed that Grandma Vi had snuck into the interview room to listen in. I was especially irritated that she could eavesdrop, but I couldn't.

Grandma Vi shook her head. "The message is loud and clear to me. Sheriff Gates has no other suspects. Pearl is going down, down, down." She flashed me an exaggerated thumbs-down.

"That's just an interrogation tactic. I don't think it's such a good idea for you to listen in on them, Grandma. It just makes things more stressful for Aunt Pearl, since she can see you. She might say the wrong thing." The combination of Grandma Vi and Pearl could stir up more trouble than I could handle. Aunt Pearl could easily break out, which was why I was here. The sooner I got my crazy aunt away from the sheriff, the better.

"Sssh. Here comes the sheriff now." Grandma retreated to the corner of the ceiling directly across from me.

Tyler Gates looked unhappy, not entirely unexpected since Aunt Pearl hadn't exactly rolled out the welcome mat for him. It was only his second day on the job and he was probably regretting it already. "I'll be keeping Pearl in custody."

I jumped to my feet. "You're arresting her?" I had promised Aunt Pearl that her interview would only take an hour or so. She would be furious with me.

"Technically no, but I'm detaining her overnight. I've got enough concerns about her personal safety that I've decided to keep her in protective custody. That way I can keep an eye on her."

I thought it was everyone else that needed to worry, but I wasn't about to say that. "She can take care of herself. But if you're worried, you can release her into my custody. I promise I'll watch her like a hawk."

Tyler shook his head slowly. "I'm afraid I can't do that. She's threatened to harm herself."

I didn't believe that for a second. I suspected Aunt Pearl's plan to end the questioning had backfired. "She's all talk. Her safety isn't enough reason to keep her in jail."

"That's not the only reason," he said. "She's too involved in the case."

I stood. "Aunt Pearl is not a murderer. I know it looks bad, but she didn't do it."

A faint smile played across Tyler Gates' lips. "I never said she did. She's being held for obstruction of justice, not murder."

"Oh." My shoulders relaxed as I absorbed the news. On the one hand I was relieved, but I also feared the havoc she could wreak from inside the police station.

"I'm sorry, but I had no choice," he said. "I'm getting pressured from the governor to solve the case, and your aunt keeps stirring up trouble. She can't just remove evidence like that."

"Oh?" I felt like a broken record, but I couldn't think of anything else to say without incriminating myself.

"Somehow she removed her cane from the evidence locker. It was securely locked up so I'm not even sure how she got in there. The lock wasn't picked and I have the only key. Pearl won't tell me how she did it, but I caught her with the evidence."

His soft brown eyes locked on mine, and I shivered despite the sweltering heat in the tiny office.

"Yes, she needs her cane."

"I suggested she get another one, but she refused. I was willing to cut her some slack, but I draw the line at interfering in a murder investigation," Sheriff Gates said.

"No, you're right to do that." I could get a lot more done without constantly chasing after Aunt Pearl. She would no doubt escape from custody, but I'd deal with that when the time came. In fact, her incarceration freed me up to do some more sleuthing on Jack and Tonya.

Tyler Gates motioned me to sit down. He took the seat beside me. "I was just talking with the coroner. Calcium oxalate crystals were found Sebastien Plant's kidneys. He had ethylene glycol poisoning." He held a manila file folder labeled *Plant - Coroner's Report* in his left hand.

My hands flew to my mouth. "I was right about the antifreeze."

He nodded. "We've got Tonya on the Walmart surveillance video around the same time as the Walmart receipt."

Finally some solid evidence that pointed towards someone other than Aunt Pearl. "So Tonya's officially a suspect now?"

"I can't say any more right now, and neither can you. I just wanted to confirm that we did follow up on the information you provided. You can't report on this until after my news release later today."

I stood, relieved that the heat would be off Aunt Pearl. "Can I go see my aunt now?" I glanced upwards but Grandma Vi had vanished. I suspected she was already commiserating with Aunt Pearl in her cell.

"I don't see why not. But remember, no mention of the coroner results yet." I promised as he beckoned me to follow him down the short hallway to the lone holding cell. Aunt Pearl sat on the bed and looked up as we approached. It was a jail cell, but it also had some homey touches like a patchwork quilt on the bed and a braided throw rug on the linoleum floor.

Aunt Pearl seemed unimpressed with the decor. She scowled as I neared the bars. "I want a lawyer."

I ignored her and stared pointedly at the sheriff.

He frowned. "Uh, right. I'll leave you two alone for a few minutes."

Westwick Corners was broke, so I was fairly certain the cell wasn't equipped with expensive cameras or listening devices. Even if we were under surveillance, I had questions that needed answering. "What's up with Tonya? You were supposed to follow her."

"That's why I was at the gas station. I followed her there but she got into a Centralex Developments truck." Aunt Pearl spat in the sink as she said the company name, like it had left a bad taste in her mouth.

"Did you see who was driving the truck?"

Aunt Pearl nodded. "It was that long-haired hippie guy that's been hanging around the hotel."

"You mean Jack Tupper? The one staying in Grandma Vi's old room?"

I was startled by a low voice cursing from above and looked up to see Grandma Vi shaking her fist and muttering to herself.

"That's the one," Aunt Pearl said. "I couldn't follow them because I was on foot. That's when the sheriff harassed me. Since when is it a crime to get gas?"

"You shouldn't have run away from him, Aunt Pearl."

"He was going to arrest me, Cen. For what?" She waved her arms. "I'm innocent. I want a lawyer."

According to the sheriff, Aunt Pearl wasn't technically arrested yet, but I didn't want to derail the discussion. "What direction was the Centralex truck headed?"

"They took the highway onramp towards Shady Creek."

My heart sank. "Now we've lost both of them. We'll never know what they're up to." Tonya and Jack each had powerful motives. Tonya had just gained sole control of the Travel Unraveled business empire, and the two of them as lovers—if that's what they were— eliminated the one roadblock to their relationship. Tonya needed to get rid of Aunt Pearl in order to move forward with her development plans, so it made perfect sense to frame Pearl for the murder.

"No need to worry." Grandma Vi descended from the ceiling and hovered beside Aunt Pearl. "I'll track them down. Where is this Centralex place? I'll start there."

I pulled out my cell phone and searched for the address. Having a ghost at my disposal was definitely an advantage. "I'm going with you."

# CHAPTER 31

*I* put the pedal to the metal and accelerated onto the highway towards Shady Creek and Centralex. I hoped that was where Tonya and Jack were headed, because I had no other way to find them.

It was hard to focus on driving with Grandma Vi floating freely around the car. Ghosts didn't sit, they hovered, and she seemed to always block my view whenever I checked the rear view mirror. Her semi-transparent form created a fog-like blurriness that made it hard to see the road in front of me too.

"Keep your eyes on the road, Cen, or you'll get us killed." Grandma hovered dangerously close to the steering wheel. I doubted a ghost could actually grab the steering wheel, but it unnerved me all the same.

"You're already dead, remember?"

"You'll be dead too if you don't slow down," she grumbled and retreated to the back seat.

I changed the subject. "Try to remember what else was going on in Tonya and Jack's room."

"You mean, besides the sex?"

"Of course, besides that. What did they talk about?"

"I wasn't really listening, but I remember something about getting hitched."

"You mean, like to each other?" Another murder motive, but I couldn't exactly give Sheriff Gates unconfirmed intelligence from an eavesdropping ghost. I had to somehow verify her claims.

"Tonya told Jack they had to wait a year till all the fuss from Sebastien's murder died down. That's all I heard."

I felt a lump in my throat at the talk of marriage. "Are you sure? Try to think back. We know one or both of them killed Sebastien Plant. We just have to prove it."

"Is that why we're chasing them all the way to Shady Creek?" Grandma hovered over the front seat, making a semi-transparent blind spot. "It seems like a waste of time. Isn't that the sheriff's job?"

"He can't deal with witches, Grandma. He needs our help."

"He did a pretty good job on Pearl. Why are we helping Sheriff Gates at all? He's locked Pearl up in the slammer. It's persecution."

"She brought that on herself and you know it." I couldn't expect Grandma Vi to be objective where her own daughter was involved. "Murder is much more serious, and Tonya and Jack are trying to get our land. We're helping our own cause. It's in our best interests to help him by setting a trap for Tonya and Jack."

"That hippie already has my room. I want him out." Grandma Vi floated sideways and hovered over the front passenger seat. "How, exactly, do we do that?"

"We say we've changed our minds about selling. I'm just the messenger for Mom, Pearl, and Amber, the real owners, so they have no choice but to return to Westwick Corners."

Grandma Vi sniffed. "It sounds risky. Don't I have a say in this?"

"Of course you do, but you're a ghost, remember? You left the property to your daughters, so it's up to them to make any deals. It's just a ruse. We aren't really going to sell the place."

"Better not. I want my room back. Especially now that you've called off the wedding."

"Fine with me." It wasn't my decision, but I wasn't willing to room with Grandma Vi on a long-term basis either. We'd drive each other nuts. "We've got to find Tonya and Jack first. We'll trick them into returning to Westwick Corners."

We drove another thirty minutes in silence until we reached the turnoff for Shady Creek. We exited the highway and drove another half-mile to downtown. Centralex occupied the tallest building, a concrete and glass monstrosity that seemed to sprout from the older low-rises of brick and wood like an invasive weed.

I slowed as we reached the building but felt a stab of fear at the idea of entering the parking lot.

"You missed the entrance," Grandma Vi pointed out.

"I know. I need to formulate a plan." I turned the corner and circled the block.

"Really, Cen? You had so much time to think about that on the drive over. Stop over-thinking and get going."

"Easy for you to say. You're invisible." I slowed the car as I returned to the front of the building. My spirits lifted when I spotted the Centralex truck in the parking lot. My hopes were just as quickly deflated when I spotted three other identical trucks. "I wish there was an easier way to find out if they're here or not."

Grandma Vi snorted. "I'll go while you wait in the car."

"Not an option." Grandma couldn't drive a car, but I had no doubt she could find trouble inside Centralex headquarters. I pulled into a spot at the far end of the parking lot and parked the car. "Let's go."

As I walked towards the building I got the sense that there was no turning back.

# CHAPTER 32

*I* pulled on the heavy glass door of Centralex headquarters, surprised to find it unlocked on a Saturday. I held it open momentarily to allow Grandma Vi to slip through. It was force of habit but completely unnecessary since she could travel through glass doors.

The main floor opened into a large glass atrium with a set of stairs along one side.

"Wait here," I said to Grandma Vi. I ascended the stairs to the second floor. I tiptoed across the thick plush carpet just as voices rose at the end of the hallway.

Two people were talking, but judging by the deep voices, it was two men—not Jack and Tonya.

I stood against the wall opposite the boardroom. My viewpoint gave me a clear line of sight through an open door to the conference table. The two men sat just ten feet away, and the one facing me was Jack.

I reeled in shock as I recognized Brayden's voice.

"The zoning has to be changed, but that's easy," Brayden said. "The councillors generally do what I say. The West family wants top dollar, but I think they'll take your offer if it's reasonably close to market value."

Something caught in my throat as I realized Brayden was talking about our property. Not only had Grandma Vi been right about Jack and Tonya's plan, but Brayden was apparently in on it too. He had been in cahoots with Jack even before our breakup. That hurt. As mayor he clearly had a conflict of interest, but how could he betray me like this?

I was so incensed that I almost marched right into the room. I took a deep breath and calmed myself as I inched closer. I didn't need Grandma Vi beside me to read Brayden's mind.

Jack slid a stack of papers across the table to Brayden. "There's something in it for you if this all gets passed."

Was Brayden being bought off? Brayden was a lot of things, but he wasn't a criminal. I was certain he wouldn't accept a cash bribe, but I also couldn't believe what I was hearing.

"I don't know," Brayden said. "It will be hard to just give up politics."

"You don't have to. Work with me for a few years and return to politics after that." Jack rose from his seat and walked around to Brayden. "You get us the political connections, and we'll make a name for you." Jack man-hugged Brayden and slapped him on the back. "Win-win."

"It's tempting," Brayden said. "There's really nothing holding me in Westwick Corners anymore."

He was obviously referring to me, but so much for the town that he also professed to love so much.

"Yeah, sorry, bro. I heard about your breakup." Jack mock-punched Brayden's arm. "You're better off in the long run."

I was infuriated that Jack had passed judgment when he didn't even know me. I disliked him more and more.

"I know." Brayden nodded.

Now I was really mad. Brayden had gotten over me awfully quick. And now he was selling out our town to the highest bidder.

While he hadn't actually done anything yet, just having this discussion with Jack made him a traitor in my eyes. As far as I knew he hadn't taken bribe money, but how was a job offer any different? Either way he was accepting a reward for turning the other way instead of looking out for the best interests of his constituents, the citizens of Westwick Corners.

I jumped as my cell phone rang. Brayden heard it too. He stepped towards the doorway and peered into the hall. His mouth dropped open as his eyes met mine.

Jack noticed me a split-second later. "Speak of the devil."

I held up my index finger. "I gotta get this." I answered the call while I scrambled to think of what to say next.

Grandma Vi's voice crackled through the air. "Where are you?"

"It doesn't matter. Why are you calling me?"

"I'm waiting for you in the lobby. Are we done yet? I want to get back to Westwick Corners." Grandma Vi closed with her most theatrical sigh.

"Ghosts don't use cell phones," I whispered into my phone as I backed away from the door as fast as I could and scurried down the hallway.

"I just called you, didn't I?"

"Where did you get my number?"

"Oh, Cen. You're just ridiculous sometimes. I don't need your number, and I don't need to call you." Grandma Vi's image slowly materialized before me. She hadn't used a phone after all, just her magic. "I had to do something to get your attention, so I pinged your ringer. I'm here to report my findings."

"What findings? You're supposed to be waiting for me downstairs."

# CHAPTER 33

"What are you doing here?" Jack's eyes narrowed as he studied me. "And why on earth are you talking to yourself?"

Grandma Vi snickered as she looked down from the ceiling.

Brayden followed Jack into the hall. "She does that all the time."

I ignored Brayden and focused on Jack. "I hope it's not too late. We've decided to sell."

"Cen, that's great." Brayden rushed towards me. "You won't regret this."

"I'm listening," Jack said. "But I've found another property so you might be too late. Or you might have to take less money for it. They are considering our offer right now."

I ignored his bluff. "Mom, Aunt Amber, and Aunt Pearl are ready to sign your documents, under one condition."

"What's that?"

"You have to return to Westwick Corners. Aunt Pearl is kind of restricted in her movements right now and can't leave town. Can you do that?"

"I suppose I could." A smile slowly spread across Jack's face.

"Great." I checked my watch. "Let's meet tomorrow morning." We needed the extra time to ensure Tonya got WICCA justice, prior to any justice served by Sheriff Gates. I walked a few steps towards the staircase and spun around. "Oh, and one more thing."

"What's that?"

"Please bring Tonya."

"Tonya Plant? Why would I bring—"

"I know all about your partnership and the resort plans." I pointed to Brayden. "Brayden told me all about it."

Jack's eyes widened. He turned to Brayden but didn't say anything.

Brayden's mouth dropped open.

"You didn't think that he would keep secrets from his future wife, did you?"

"I didn't tell her anything." Brayden turned to Jack. "I don't know what she's talking about. I haven't told a soul."

I shrugged and turned towards the stairs with Grandma Vi a few feet ahead. I descended the steps, feeling nauseous that I had been so gullible. Like a fool I had placed my complete trust in Brayden, oblivious to the fact he had never been loyal to me in the first place. I just hoped Grandma wouldn't make a big deal about being right. I wasn't in the mood for it.

Grandma Vi hovered impatiently by the door. "Hurry up, we haven't got all day."

\* \* \*

"What's wrong with you?" I glanced over at Grandma Vi, who was uncharacteristically silent as we cruised down the highway towards Westwick Corners. "You're awfully quiet."

Grandma Vi just shrugged as she hovered above the passenger seat. She hadn't strayed from her position since leaving Shady Creek a half hour ago. It made driving easier but worried me all the same. Something wasn't right.

I didn't press her, deciding to just enjoy the quiet for a change. It was a bright, sunny day, perfect for a scenic drive. I might as well enjoy it before I had to face Jack and Tonya again.

A sharp banging noise coming from the rear of the car startled me. I didn't know much about cars but I vaguely remembered a loose exhaust pipe on my old car once. This noise didn't have quite the same rattle, but it was all I could think of. Maybe it was a loose exhaust pipe or something. "I'm pulling over. I think something on the car is broken."

"No, no, no!" Grandma Vi waved her arms frantically. "Keep going!"

"I can't. Not when my car is falling apart." I slowed and pulled over to the right lane.

"Cen, listen to me." Grandma Vi floated two inches from my face. Transparent or not, I could barely see in front of me. It was like driving in heavy fog, only it was a bright sunny day outside. "Tonya's in the trunk."

The car lurched as the passenger side left the pavement. It landed with a thud on the soft gravel shoulder.

I raised one hand off the steering wheel to push her away but naturally my hand went right through her. "Get out of my way, Grandma! I can't see a thing."

She scooted back to the passenger seat. "Oops, sorry."

"Why didn't you tell me this earlier?" It was now clear as day that the rattling noise was a knocking sound coming from the trunk.

"I didn't want to scare you, because then you'd just slow down and we'd end up...just like we are now."

"I see." But I didn't see at all. "Tonya's a witch. Can't she use magic to escape the trunk?"

"Not against my magic, but we don't have much time. My ghost witch spells don't last very long at all. I figure we've got another five or ten minutes before the magic wears off. Now get back on the highway and gun it."

"I don't understand. Tonya would have come anyway—"

"Cen, shut your mouth." Grandma shook her head back and forth.

"What?"

Grandma Vi made a zipping motion across her mouth and tapped the side of her head.

Of course. Since Grandma could read minds, I could just think my questions. That way Tonya wouldn't hear them. But wouldn't she hear Grandma's answers? Maybe the spell dealt with that somehow.

Grandma Vi turned up the radio full blast and mouthed her words. "Before Tonya and Jack answer to their crimes in Westwick Corners, Tonya has to face WICCA justice. She's committed super-natural crimes too, and those must be dealt with first."

At least that's what I thought she said. "So you kidnapped her?" Grandma Vi's brand of justice made me a little uneasy, and I couldn't for the life of me figure out how she got Tonya in the trunk. It was physically impossible. Grandma Vi obviously had some tricks up her ghostly sleeve.

"I did nothing of the sort. She had a warrant." She grinned. "And a decent bounty on her head too."

# CHAPTER 34

*A*unt Pearl was already waiting for us when we pulled up in front of Pearl's Charm School. She had taken a supernatural unauthorized leave of absence from the Westwick County Jail to see justice served. I just hoped the sheriff didn't check in on her for a few hours. We had WICCA business to take care of.

"Hazel's gone ahead to set things up at WICCA's London office," Aunt Pearl said. WICCA justice was swift, but plenty could go wrong until we delivered Tonya to face the tribunal.

Alan ran towards us, tail wagging. "We're bringing Alan."

Aunt Pearl shook her head. "Now's not the time, Cen."

"Yes, it is exactly the right time."

"She's right, Pearl." Grandma Vi motioned to the car trunk where Tonya was kicking and screaming inside. "You've got no time to waste. You two better go."

My eyes widened. The thought of Aunt Pearl and me keeping Tonya in check terrified me. Of course we had Alan, but his abilities were limited in his current form. "You're not coming with us?"

Grandma Vi shook her head. "Now that I'm back home, I don't intend to leave again no matter what. Now hurry."

We removed a cursing Tonya from the trunk and huddled together. Alan's warning growls kept Tonya in check.

I followed Aunt Pearl's teleportation instructions, and less than five minutes later we all rematerialized in front of a steel and concrete high-rise. It was well lit despite the fact that it was obviously well after midnight. The downtown streets were silent and devoid of people. It was spooky, to say the least.

The revolving front door began spinning ever so slowly. I assumed that was an invitation to enter so we did, Aunt Pearl in front, Tonya in the middle, and me bringing up the rear. We entered an elevator that seemed to pop up right in front of us. The door closed and Aunt Pearl pressed the button for the sixty-seventh floor.

We rode in silence, Aunt Pearl's earlier words about Tonya being a lousy witch giving me comfort until I realized my aunt probably said exactly the same thing about me.

The elevator doors opened and we were greeted by two burly security guards. One took Tonya down the hall to a holding room. The second guard ushered us into the main office. I followed behind Aunt Pearl and Alan towards the WICCA council conference room.

Witches International Community Craft Association was a centuries-old global organization, so I had imagined Witch Hazel's London office to be dark paneled wood and brick, housed in a drafty old mansion with massive stone fireplaces.

It was exactly the opposite. Rather than mystical and cozy, the office decor was clean, sterile, and modern, befitting the sixty-seventh floor of London's tallest office building. The furnishings were modern, sparse, and white, with lots of chrome, glass, and high-wattage lighting. Like everything else, WICCA changed with the times.

My romantic, mystical image of WICCA had developed because I knew very little about it. In fact, I had always tried to ignore WICCA and anything to do with my supernatural self, but Aunt Pearl's magic lessons had opened up a whole new world to me, a world I never wanted to really see until now.

I also saw my aunt in a whole new light. Yes, she was ornery and stubborn, but she also cared deeply for Westwick Corners and would do anything to protect the town and our way of life. She also took her talents very seriously. I would never admit it, but I was proud of her.

Aunt Pearl and I were the two key witnesses testifying against Tonya, and I didn't want to mess things up. We had a huge task ahead of us. Magic infractions had to be tried under the WICCA justice system. I just hoped that our claims withstood supernatural scrutiny.

Aunt Amber ushered us into the executive boardroom where Hazel was already seated at the head of the white lacquer board-room table. Aunt Amber took a seat to the left of Hazel, and Aunt Pearl and I sat beside her.

Hazel remained seated and said nothing. From her tired expression and bloodshot, swollen eyes, it was obvious she had been crying. Because of her relationship with Sebastien she couldn't be part of the hearing; however, as WICCA president she was required to be present.

Alan followed behind me and sat at my feet. I was determined to defeat Hazel's excuses and procrastination. One look into his soulful brown eyes would guilt Hazel into changing him back to his human form, but it had to wait until the hearing was over.

I shifted my gaze to the opposite side of the boardroom table to the three judges who would decide Tonya's fate. The three frail, gray-haired women appeared to be at least in their nineties. They all had a wrinkled, learned look, which I hoped meant they were very wise in terms of WICCA law.

Supernatural beings required supernatural deterrents. That was the reason WICCA dispensed its own justice and why our mission was so critical.

The tension-filled room was a powder keg of emotions ready to ignite as Tonya was escorted in by a security guard. She looked down, avoiding eye contact with anyone as the first judge read out the charges against her.

The most serious charge, Abuse of Supernatural Powers, had the most severe punishment. If found guilty, Tonya would be expelled from WICCA and forever stripped of her supernatural powers.

Mortal punishments paled against WICCA ones, and a Washington jail cell was nothing compared to WICCA sentences. If Tonya were found innocent in the WICCA court, her supernatural powers would remain intact. She would easily escape a Washington State prison and get away with her crimes. That was why she had to be tried under WICCA law first. All we had to do was provide proof that Tonya had committed a crime using witchcraft. Proof of the crime was easy, since we had ample evidence that she had killed her husband. The harder part was showing how she had used her supernatural powers to do so.

"First witness," Judge Number One said. "State your name and address."

My palms dampened with sweat as I recited my details. I gradually relaxed as I summarized the facts, starting with finding Sebastien Plant's body in the gazebo and ending with the discovery of antifreeze in Sebastien's glass on the bedside table.

Judge Number Two wrung her pale, blue-veined hands together. "That's all you've got? No magic involved in any of that."

"No, there's more." The future of Westwick Corners depended on my last piece of evidence. Was it enough?

I pulled three copies of the coroner's report from my bag. I had used my magic to make copies of the coroner's report, making me just as bad as Aunt Pearl. It was to ensure justice was served, I told myself as I gave a copy to each judge. "The coroner's report proves that Tonya poisoned Sebastien before Jack hit him with the tire iron. Sebastien had already ingested the poison when he and Tonya checked in, but she gave him even more in their room. Her fingerprints are on the glass, and his DNA is on the rim of the glass. Based on the coroner's estimates, he drank the lethal dose of antifreeze sometime after they checked in. Pearl can corroborate the check in time. Yet he didn't arrive at the gazebo until hours later. He would have lost the ability to stand, let alone walk, by then."

I glanced at the judges to gauge their reaction, but their faces remained expressionless. Aunt Pearl squirmed in her seat beside me. "Someone had to carry three-hundred-pound Sebastien Plant to the gazebo."

I drew a deep breath and pulled out my last weapon, my laptop. On it was surveillance footage from our security camera. "You can see Tonya and Sebastien floating outside the Inn."

Tonya shot to her feet. "That doesn't prove a thing."

"It proves you were outside with Sebastien, not sleeping as you claimed. The camera footage is from 7:30 a.m., and if you look closely, you can see that Sebastien's eyes are closed. He is very clearly unconscious."

The judges' faces remained impassive as they watched the surveillance video.

"It also proves that Tonya used her supernatural powers to get him to the gazebo." I turned and locked eyes with all three judges, who leaned forward in unison.

The video didn't lie. But it proved that Tonya had.

"Tonya tried to frame Pearl, another WICCA member, for the crime. But she gave herself away with the note she left at the scene." I pulled out a copy of the note and slid it across the table to the judges. "She spelled unraveled with two Ls".

Judge Three's brows knitted together in confusion. "So she can't spell, so what?"

"It's not an error, Judge. Pearl is American and uses the American spelling, which has only one L."

"Lots of people use British spelling. Hazel, for instance," Tonya protested. "That alone doesn't make me guilty."

I shook my head. "Hazel couldn't rhyme if her life depended on it."

Hazel glared at me, even though I had just vouched for her. "The crime lab analyzed the note and Tonya's fingerprints were all over it. Hazel's weren't." I slid the report across the table.

Judge Two grabbed it with a boney hand.

Aunt Pearl sighed. "I've already spent time in the slammer because of Tonya's false accusation. I want justice served."

Judge Three gasped. "Tonya tried to frame another WICCA member?"

I nodded. "She also convinced Jack that he had murdered Plant. When he delivered the tire iron blows, he had no idea that Tonya had already given Sebastien a lethal dose of ethylene glycol, or antifreeze."

Hazel gasped.

"How do you plead, Witch Tonya?" Judge Number One asked.

"Guilty."

# CHAPTER 35

*I* awoke early and headed to my office, refreshed after a good night's sleep and the knowledge that Tonya Plant had been stripped of her supernatural powers. The three WICCA judges' decision had been unanimous. Tonya's supernatural powers had been immediately and permanently stripped, and she would serve a ten-year WICCA sentence once her Washington state sentence ended.

Justice was served for Alan, too. Hazel had removed her curse and returned my brother to his human form. He was back to his normal self, having a very hearty breakfast at the Inn.

Tonya had been released awaiting sentencing under the condition she wore an ankle monitoring bracelet so that her whereabouts would be known at all times. I had no doubt that she was with Jack, en route to Westwick Corners at this very moment.

I was confident she would return, since she was practically salivating about her Westwick Corners vortex resort. She was certain that, despite the WICCA conviction, her plan would all still come together. All she and Jack needed was to finalize the paperwork with us for a done deal.

I had something else in mind based on the evidence now in Sheriff Gates' possession. I could hardly wait to see Tonya and Jack arrested and justice served, and our ruse to accept their sale offer would finally expose them.

While I awaited their arrival, I needed to finalize the current issue of *The Westwick Corners Weekly*. And what a week it had been. A murder, a canceled wedding (that kind of thing was headline news in our town), a conflicted mayor, and finally, news that we had our very own vortex. Who knew?

Then there was the other news I couldn't print that was rocketing through the witch world: one of our own had been responsible for a horrific crime and was about to pay the price. That story didn't need anything from me. It pretty much wrote itself.

My original feature on the Westwick Corners Inn's grand opening seemed trivial compared to the other news, so I had no choice but to kill that story and replace it with one on Sebastien Plant's murder. The lost publicity would probably hurt our business, but the other news would more than make up for it.

For once, *The Westwick Corners Weekly* would be full of original content rather than coupons and advertorials. People would get the facts before the story was spun and embellished by the rumor mill. And, I realized, the stories were really one and the same.

In short, Westwick Corners was an interesting place and well worth a detour off the highway. Tourists were unlikely to read our local paper, but locals who did would certainly flock to *The Witching Post* to discuss the latest happenings over drinks. I could make good out of a bad situation.

I glanced at my watch and realized that our scheduled meeting with Jack and Tonya was in less than thirty minutes. They thought they were about to buy our property, but we had something completely different in mind.

That is, if I made it to the Inn on time.

Desperate times called for desperate measures, so I used magic to draft a story about the murder, another one about the Plants and their company, Travel Unraveled. Add in a vortex and voilà, I had a final edition.

A half hour later the paper was proofed, formatted, and ready to be published. All I had left to do was upload the story to *The Westwick Corners Weekly* website at the appropriate time.

I had just sipped my cold coffee when a large bang startled me.

"What the—?" I choked, spewing the liquid all over my desk.

A split second later an airborne Aunt Pearl dropped through the ceiling and into the office chair opposite my desk. Despite her small stature, the chair cracked from velocity of the impact. Ninety pounds of skin and bone will do that from eight feet high. Aunt Pearl herself looked no worse for wear.

"Damn! I'm getting too old for this." She winced as she wiggled her bum in the seat. "Jack and Tonya have just arrived at the Inn. Why are you still here?"

Aunt Pearl had been officially cleared of all suspicion this morning, after the coroner's report identified the tire iron as the murder weapon. The blood on her wand had been cow's blood, not human. The whole thing had been staged to frame her, but forensics proved otherwise.

"Sorry." I stood and followed behind my aunt as she headed for the door.

"Just remember to follow my lead." She skipped down the stairs, tapping her wand on the railing as she descended. "Damn, it feels good to be free."

I flashed back to my almost wedding and my almost life as a politician's wife. "I couldn't agree more."

# CHAPTER 36

$\mathcal{M}$om, Aunt Pearl, and I followed behind Tonya and Jack as we headed across the garden to the gazebo. Tonya Plant and Jack Tupper III were reluctant participants, duped into the premise of Aunt Pearl's arrest at the scene of the crime for Sebastien Plant's murder.

While both Tonya and Jack were eager to see Aunt Pearl arrested for murder, they were even more enthusiastic about getting the paperwork signed for the sale of our property.

I tapped my watch. "Aunt Amber was supposed to arrive an hour ago. I'm sure she'll be here any minute." It was a lie, designed to stall them.

"That will have to wait," Sheriff Gates walked towards us. "I've got some business of my own to take care of. I've got some questions that need answering about Sebastien." Tyler pointed to Tonya, who ignored him. She stood several feet back from the group, immersed in something on her smartphone screen.

Jack cleared his throat and fidgeted with his hands.

It took Tonya a moment to realize that everyone was staring at her. "You can't be serious. It's a wonder you got hired as sheriff, even in this little hick town. You do realize that nobody else would take the job here."

Sheriff Gates ignored the insult.

"Most people wouldn't even want to live here," Tonya added. "Even incompetent cops."

Pearl's eyes narrowed. "This so-called hick town is on a vortex, missy. You're just jealous you can't live here. If you think you're taking over our vortex, you've got another thing coming."

Mom patted Pearl's arm. "Settle down, Pearl. The vortex is for everyone to enjoy."

"But not to take over and exploit," I added.

Sheriff Gates looked confused. "What vortex?"

I waved my hand in dismissal. "I'll explain later."

"Whatever." Tonya scowled at the sheriff. "I knew this would be a waste of time. I've got to go, so I'll leave the paperwork with you. Any questions can be handled through my assistant." She rummaged through her purse and extracted a business card. She shoved it into the sheriff's hand.

"You're not going anywhere," he said.

"You can't order me around. I'm free to do as I please. You're too incompetent to ever find my husband's killer."

The sheriff ignored the insult. "You're under arrest for the murder of Sebastien Plant."

"That's ridiculous. I've got an alibi. They all saw me at the inn." She waved her hand dismissively at Mom, Aunt Pearl, and me. "I was with them, dealing with their abysmal customer service at the time of the murder."

"I don't recall seeing you," Aunt Pearl said.

I made a cutting motion across my neck. The one thing my aunt excelled at was getting everyone riled up and off topic. That was the last thing we needed right now.

"I doubt you remember much of anything, you old bag." Tonya slung her purse over her shoulder and motioned for Jack to follow.

I recalled Aunt Pearl's comment about Tonya being older than she looked. Why didn't she look that way if she had been stripped of her powers? Maybe there was a delay before it took effect.

"You have no right to talk to me that way!" Aunt Pearl held her wand in the air and was just about to use it before I stopped her from another criminal charge.

Thankfully Tonya ignored her. She turned to Jack. "Let's go."

Jack frowned but turned and followed on Tonya's heels.

"Hold up," Sheriff Gates said. "You can't leave until I say so. You both have plenty to answer for."

"The hell with that," Tonya said. "You can talk to my lawyer. I was at the Inn the whole time, so you can't blame me for Sebastien's murder.

So much for the grieving widow.

"Aaah, but that wasn't when the murder happened. Sebastien Plant died much earlier, and during that time you had no alibi. You were alone for an hour, starting from when Sebastien took his walk, until later when you met Jack in his room."

"That's not true. I never left my room. These ladies can confirm I was inside the Inn the whole time. Isn't that right?"

She stared at me so I nodded. "You never went outside with Sebastien for a walk."

"See, sheriff. You couldn't solve a murder if your life depended on it. It's obvious to everyone that Pearl West killed my husband with her cane. Anything else is just ridiculous." Tonya punched in some numbers on her phone. "I'm calling the governor. I want you removed from the case immediately."

"No one's removing me from the case, because the case is solved." Tyler's eyes met mine in a silent thank you as he pulled out handcuffs. "You're under arrest for the murder of Sebastien Plant."

He read Tonya her rights but didn't cuff her right away.

"Right to remain silent, my ass." Tonya glared at him and turned sideways. She yelled into her phone, but whoever answered the governor's calls was apparently screening them. "Put me through to him right now or I'll get you fired."

Hardly the behavior of a mourning spouse, I thought.

"Shut that thing off." Tyler waved the handcuffs in front of her face. "The only person you should be calling right now is a lawyer."

Tonya glared at him but finally listened. She stood silent and crossed her arms if only to delay the inevitable handcuffs.

"You might not have delivered the blow, but you did kill your husband. Most of the time it's the spouse, and this time isn't any different."

"You really are an idiot." For the first time Tonya's face showed a hint of fear.

"Sebastien suffered blunt force trauma, but it wasn't Pearl's cane that did it." Tyler Gates scanned our faces. "His attacker is right here."

"It's obviously Pearl," muttered Tonya. "She was even stupid enough to leave her cane behind."

"How dare you call me stupid!" Aunt Pearl raised her cane in the air and started towards Tonya.

"She's at it again," Tonya cried. "Stop her!"

I grabbed my aunt from behind in a bear hug and pulled her back. I realized that I couldn't remember ever hugging her. She just wasn't really the touchy-feely type. It was like I was seeing her for the first time though. My aunt was just so full of spunk and vinegar that I hadn't realized how tiny or fragile she really was.

"Pearl didn't kill him," Tyler said. "She's not strong enough to apply that much force."

I glanced nervously at Mom. Pearl had plenty of strength with her supernatural powers. Tonya was well aware of that too. Was she desperate enough to reveal we were witches?

"Actually, she can—"

I cut Tonya off before she could finish her sentence. "Pearl's obviously no match for a three-hundred-pound man."

"Especially not one over six feet tall," Tyler added. "She couldn't reach high enough to hit him on the top of the head. And there's just no way she has enough strength to disable him."

Aunt Pearl's eyes narrowed as she scowled at the sheriff.

"Can I go now?" Tonya snapped.

Tyler Gates ignored both of them. "Whatever struck Sebastien's head was much heavier than Pearl's cane. His attacker was also strong enough to leave an imprint not just on his skin but also cracks on his skull."

We all turned to look at Jack, who, at over six feet, towered over Tonya. His eyes widened as Alan stepped out of the gazebo. At six-foot-two, he looked rather intimidating next to Jack. He smiled, ready to assist the sheriff if needed.

Tyler Gates' left hand held handcuffs. "In fact, we know exactly what his attacker used." He bent down and picked up a tire iron beside the gazebo steps. "A tire iron, exactly like this one. The end of this tire iron left a distinct impression on Sebastien Plant's skull. An impression that doesn't match Pearl's cane. It does however, exactly match the tire iron from Jack's Lamborghini."

"You can't prove that." Jack broke out into a cold sweat. "It could have been anything."

Sheriff Gates shook his head. "The imprint on Sebastien's temple is very clear. I got a warrant to search your car this morning. Your tire iron was missing."

Jack breathed an audible sigh of relief.

"That is, until we recovered it from the trash can in your room. The blood on it was Sebastien's."

"That's a lie. Pearl's cane was covered in blood too."

Tyler dismissed him with a wave of his hand. "You stole Pearl's cane and left it at the gazebo to implicate her. The imprint on Sebastien's temple eliminates her cane. Not only that, but the angle and force required to make that imprint could only be done by someone much taller than Pearl. In fact, you're the only one at the Inn last night that meets the height requirement."

"He's the guy I saw!" Pearl's hands flew to her mouth. "The guy in the hoodie."

Tonya shrieked. "You killed my husband!" She charged Jack and pounded his chest with her fists.

The sheriff fixated on Jack. "You followed him to the gazebo and hit him over the head."

"No way, I wasn't there."

"You don't have an alibi. Besides, we have an eyewitness."

"I want a lawyer," Jack said. "I had nothing to do with this."

"Jack was so jealous of Sebastien." Tonya's shrieks were replaced by dead calm. "Jack insisted I leave him, but I refused. So he killed my poor, sweet, husband."

"That's a lie," Jack cried. "You told me you wanted him out of your life. That he beat you."

"I said no such thing. You're just obsessed with me." Tonya wiped a pretend tear from her dry cheek. "Seb and I had a happy life together. Cut short by a monster."

"It doesn't matter all that much in the end," Tyler said. "The blunt force trauma isn't what killed him."

"It didn't?" Jack seemed suddenly hopeful.

Tyler shook his head. "Sebastien was poisoned. Jack's hit just disguised the true cause of death."

"No, Jack killed him. I demand you arrest him right now," Tonya cried.

I suddenly noticed four Shady Creek police officers walking across the garden. They waited about ten feet away as Sheriff Gates talked. They had probably been brought in as reinforcements.

"Sebastien Plant died from ethyl glycol poisoning. In fact, he was already dead when Jack hit him with the tire iron. That's why there wasn't much blood," Sheriff Gates said. "It's also why the tire iron left such a distinct impression on his skull. The coroner said that if he was still alive with his blood circulating, the tire iron's imprint wouldn't have been so distinct."

Aunt Pearl scoffed. "That woman has a whole bag of tricks up her sleeve. What a witch."

I flinched from her reference, but no one else seemed to take notice.

Sheriff Gates pointed to Tonya. "You concocted this elaborate scene to frame Jack for the murder. That's why you checked in early and kept Sebastien in his room until he could barely walk. Sebastien wasn't drunk, he was poisoned. You persuaded him to go outside for some fresh air and walk off his drunkenness. You had to, because there was no way to carry an obese, three-hundred-pound man."

"Why take him to the gazebo at all?" Alan asked.

"He was hidden from view. It bought her time so that he wouldn't be discovered too soon. The antifreeze effects can be reversed, but there's only a small window of time before it's too late. She couldn't leave him in her room without explaining why she didn't call for help. Claiming he took a walk in the garden was perfect. She has an alibi while he was slowly dying."

"It's all my fault." Tonya's voice broke. "He was very depressed and I never should have left him alone. He was having suicidal thoughts the last few months. But I had no idea he drank antifreeze."

"Most people don't know that ethyl glycol is the chemical name for the main ingredient in antifreeze, yet you seem awfully familiar with it."

"That's because I'm a smart person, Sheriff. Just wish I was smart enough to stop my husband from taking his own life."

"I'm quite confident you helped him," Tyler said. "Someone put the ethylene glycol in his drink. We tested the glass on the night-stand in your suite and found traces of the chemical. Your fingerprints were on the glass. You must have slipped it in his drink."

"That's some imagination you've got, Sheriff. But that's not what happened."

"No one commits suicide with antifreeze," Sheriff Gates replied. "They take pills or put a gun to their head. There are other things we found that are inconsistent with suicide. Oddly enough, while Sebastien's glass had your fingerprints, his were missing. You held the glass to Sebastien's lips while he was barely conscious and forced him to drink it. Suicidal people don't wear gloves to hide their fingerprints. They don't care about stuff like that, because they no longer care about anything once they decide to check out."

"Your crime lab is probably just as incompetent as you," Tonya said. "You missed his prints or got the wrong glass."

She sounded more desperate by the minute.

"It's the state crime lab. This is just one of many cases they handle, and they've got a pretty good reputation. I'll pass on your feedback to the crime lab and the governor too."

"If he was actually poisoned, how could he even walk, let alone travel all the way to the gazebo?" Tonya fake-sobbed.

"Easily. The poison effects from the antifreeze aren't instantaneous. The first signs are when a person slurs their words and loses coordination."

"Like a drunk," Mom said.

"Exactly," Tyler said. "The poison became apparent during the autopsy. Ethylene glycol forms crystals in the kidneys that remain intact after death. That was the cause of death. The blunt force trauma from Jack's tire iron was severe, but it happened later. In any event, it wasn't enough to cause instantaneous death."

Jack's brows furrowed together as he studied Tonya. "You lied to me. You made up all those lies about Sebastien. You just used me."

Tyler looked pointedly at Jack. "That's exactly what she did. She framed you for Sebastien's murder."

Aunt Pearl nodded. For once she was on the sheriff's side. "Always suspect the spouse, no matter what."

Tonya scowled as Sheriff Gates placed the cuffs on her wrists. Another officer did the same for Jack, and the two were led away to the waiting police cars to be transported to the Shady Creek jail.

We stood in silence as we watched them.

"I'm glad that's over," Mom said.

"It's over for you but just starting for Tonya," Tyler said. "Sebastien wasn't Tonya's first husband—or the first one to die under suspicious circumstances either. Her first husband died suddenly at age thirty-eight. His family wanted an autopsy but as next-of-kin, Tonya refused. I suspect they'll be exhuming his body."

The witch who had everything had just lost it all.

# CHAPTER 37

$\mathcal{I}$ was completely exhausted from my almost wedding, break up, Plant's murder, and overseas WICCA tribunal over the course of a single weekend. Judging from her expression, so was Aunt Pearl.

"Pearl's Charm School is on semester break, effective now," she said.

"Did I pass?" I asked.

"You barely even got started." Aunt Pearl smirked. "But for the little you did do, I haven't finalized the marks yet."

My mouth dropped open. After everything I had done, I thought I deserved an A-plus. "I should get an automatic pass."

"Just messing with ya, Cen. You'll pass."

I relaxed, surprised at how much my magic, and Aunt Pearl's approval, suddenly meant to me. I felt a new affection for my aunt now that I realized how much she had risked to save our town. We might have more in common than I had originally thought.

We sat at a large picnic table in the rear garden. A warm afternoon breeze rustled through the leaves of the tall aspen trees that bordered the rear of our property. The last of the weekend guests had departed a few hours ago, so we took advantage of the nice weather to hold an impromptu barbecue.

Our stomachs were full with barbecued chicken, Mom's secret recipe potato salad, and fresh corn on the cob. Aunt Pearl and I sat across from Hazel and Aunt Amber who had arrived in Westwick Corners just in time to celebrate Tonya's capture. We had also invited Sheriff Gates to join us. He sat on Aunt Amber's right.

Tyler looked up suddenly as Alan ran across the lawn towards us. Though back in human form, he had kept his canine energy level and his appetite seemed larger than ever. He grinned ear to ear as he walked toward the table. I smiled back, feeling his infectious happiness as he joined us at the table. I was almost as relieved as he was.

While Alan was kind of fun in his Border collie form, I had to admit I had been a little worried that he might never change back. I had missed him too. It was nice to have my brother back. Even Hazel seemed happy for him. It was especially good to see that Hazel and Aunt Pearl were fast friends once again.

"Hope you've got room for desert." Mom emerged from the back door of the kitchen with a large tray. My heart sank as soon as I saw the wedding cake. I had momentarily forgotten my canceled wedding and breakup with Brayden, but the cake brought all those feelings back. Suddenly the day seemed clouded with guilt.

"Time for a celebration."

Everyone turned to look at me as Mom placed the cake on the table.

"Mom, no." I shook my head.

"Relax, Cen. This is a perfectly good cake and I'm not letting it go to waste. Take a closer look." Mom waved a hand at the top of the cake.

My shoulders sagged as I focused on the cake. My spirits lifted as I saw that while it was my wedding cake, the decorations were completely different. The bride and groom atop the cake had been replaced by a miniature rendition of the Westwick Corners Inn, complete with the entire West family.

Mom, Pearl, and Amber stood on the front porch, arm in arm. Alan (in his human form) and I stood in front of the house, while Grandma Vi floated a few inches above us. My heart warmed at the sentimental scene that Mom had so painstakingly recreated atop the cake.

Even Mom couldn't work that fast without magic though, so she must have used some. I guess we both felt more confident about our talents. I felt a surge of affection for my super-cool talented mom, who was crafty and thrifty all at the same time. I also felt a huge debt of gratitude as I realized she had single-handedly kept everything at the Inn running smoothly while Aunt Pearl and I fought supernatural crime. "It's beautiful. I don't think I can ruin it by eating it."

"Don't be silly, Cen." Mom handed me the knife. "Now make a wish."

A few ideas flashed through my mind, but for the first time I felt like I really didn't want for anything.

I wouldn't change a thing about my dead-end job at my barely solvent newspaper. I wasn't even sure if I wanted to change Westwick Corners anymore. I loved my eccentric family just the way they were, regardless of what outsiders thought. I even loved me. For the first time I was proud to be a witch. I would never take anything I had for granted ever again.

I glanced around the table. All eyes focused on me, waiting for me to slice the cake. My eyes locked onto the sexy brown eyes of Tyler Gates.

My heart did a somersault.

I closed my eyes and took a deep breath.

Maybe I did have a wish after all.

\* \* \*

LOVE *WITCH YOU WELL?* Read the next Westwick Witches book, *Rags to Witches*

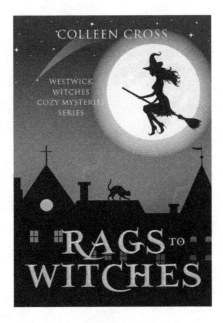

# AFTERWORD

If you enjoyed reading *Witch You Well,* please consider leaving a short review or recommending it to a friend. Word of mouth is an author's best friend and the feedback lets me know whether to continue a series or not.

*Witch You Well* is the first book in the Westwick Witches Cozy Mysteries series and I have many more books planned for this paranormal cozy mystery series. As long as readers like you enjoy my stories, I will continue to write them.

If you loved *Witch You Well* and want to know about new releases, sign up for my newsletter. Emails are sent for new releases only so you'll only get notified when I've written something new—nothing else! You'll also be the first to know when a new book is out! Sign up at www.colleencross.com

I have also several other mystery and thriller series that you might enjoy. Links to my other books are on the next page.

Thank you so much for reading!

*Colleen Cross*

# ALSO BY COLLEEN CROSS

Westwick Witches Cozy Mysteries

*Witch You Well*

*Rags to Witches*

*Witch and Famous*

*Christmas Witch List*

*Witching Hour Dead*

*Witching for Love on Valentines Day*

Katerina Carter Fraud Legal Thrillers

*Exit Strategy*

*Game Theory*

*Blowout*

*Greenwash*

*Red Handed*

*Blue Moon*

Nonfiction

*Anatomy of a Ponzi Scheme*

CPSIA information can be obtained
at www.ICGtesting.com
Printed in the USA
LVHW102050090722
723113LV00017B/260

9 781663 574084